PROLOGUE
BETWEEN

FORGIVE ME, FATHER, FOR I have sinned.

They whispered the words in their head, drew the imaginary cross against their chest.

And then they cleared their throat and confessed their sins.

At first, the priest said nothing, and time stood still. The two of them sat there, suffocating in the silence of the tiny boxes, the gravity of the situation striking in full force.

You shouldn't have done this.

Now he knows.

You're not worthy of forgiveness.

A bead of sweat broke out on the tip of their hairline, their heartbeat speeding up in a storm of anxiety.

If he doesn't respond soon, I'll have to—

And then the priest spoke, halting the onslaught of dangerous thoughts.

"May God, who is wonderful and rich in mercy, hear the sins of your heart and forgive you, child."

A smile and tear simultaneously loosed, instantly transforming their face.

I am free.

ISLA
NOW

THE SHARP EDGES OF the coffin reflected in Isla's gaze.

Breathe.

Not exactly how she'd planned to kick off the holidays, especially as a business owner, yet here she was, standing inside the oversized sanctuary of a massive Catholic church in her hometown of Wilderby, West Virginia, staring at her ex-best friend's casket.

It'd been three days since she got the call about Rebecca's death. She'd been standing in the storage closet at her coffee shop, attempting to carry way too many bags of flour, and had dropped them all, coating herself and the room in a sea of white dust. *Head injury, freak accident, subdural hematoma, nothing they could do.* The memories played on repeat as she took another step, wondering how long Rebecca had been dead, lying there on the basement floor of her house before her roommate found her.

The line moved, and Isla shuddered, trying to expunge the thought. She took a steadying breath and prepared herself for what was next. She'd been to several funerals before, but they were always for older people—grandparents, great aunts, a friendly neighbor. She'd never seen the dead body of someone her own age, much less someone so close to her.

Someone she considered a friend, a soul sister. *A source of trauma.*

A man behind Isla coughed, and she knew that was her cue to move, to step forward and visit the front of the casket, *paying her respects.* The thought sent a rigid chill down her spine, causing her skin to tingle.

You can do this.

You have to do this.

Nodding, she walked toward the midnight-colored coffin, fear stabbing in her throat. Slowly, Rebecca's body came into view, and Isla shuddered. Becca had always been thin due to both genetics and an eating disorder, but the mere skeletal figure lying inside the satin-lined box was almost unrecognizable.

Sweet Becca, she thought. *You deserved so much more.*

Digging her nails into the palms of her hands, Isla trailed her gaze up Rebecca's corpse, skimming over her auburn hair and landing on her face. Isla took in Becca's swollen eye sockets, busted lips, and ruptured varicose veins, all while a thunderous crack vibrated in her chest. She couldn't comprehend why Becca's mom had opted for an open casket ceremony when she looked like this.

Unable to stare at this version of her old friend any longer, Isla cleared her throat and blew a kiss, letting the gesture melt away into an "I love you" sign. Her heart squeezed as she realized Rebecca wasn't going to wake and return their signature signal, so Isla swallowed the lump in her throat and flew past the receiving line. She reached one of the wooden pews in the center of the room and settled into an empty spot.

Deep breaths, Isla.

SECRET SANTA

AMY TACKETT

Cover Design by Ink and Laurel

Edited by Impress Millenial Books

Proofread by Kaylynn Wurzelbacher

Printed in the United States of America

ISBN 979-8-9886589-1-7 (Paperback)

This ain't your grandma's Christmas book—nothing holly or jolly 'bout it. To view a complete list of content warnings, please visit my website.

OFFICIAL PLAYLIST

"Bury a Friend" — Billie Eilish

"I'll Fly Away" — Alan Jackson

"Deck da Club" — Ying Yang Twins

"I Know Places" — Taylor Swift

"Spooky Christmas" — Mark Russell

"Hallelujah" — Pentatonix

"Fancy" — Iggy Azalea

"Bad Guy" — Billie Eilish

"Chocolate" — The 1975

"Mad Woman" — Taylor Swift

"Mistletoe" — Justin Bieber

"Secret" — The Pierces

"Blurred Lines" — Robin Thicke

"Silent Night" — Pentatonix

"Look What You Made Me Do" — Taylor Swift

"Christmas Eve / Sarajevo" — Trans-Siberian Orchestra

To the original Everclear Kids and the later renowned Fire Tribe.

Thnks fr th Mmrs.

"Mean girls would have little power if it weren't for their enablers—that is, the rest of us."

—Deb Landry, *The Mean Girl Phenomenon; Understanding Relational Aggression*

PART I

Needing a distraction, she cast a glance at the other guests. Although she hadn't lived in Wilderby for nearly a decade, Isla recognized several faces. Mr. Joss, their high school English teacher, stood at the front of the line, flanked by an onslaught of other faculty members. Next was Darcy Jones, owner of Thick Chicks, the town's go-to bar and restaurant—and coincidentally, the place where Rebecca worked until her death. Even at thirty-one, she was still slinging beers to country bumpkins and wannabe lumberjacks.

Trailer trash, her mind whispered.

Isla's skin prickled as shame encompassed her. Because that's what they'd called Becca when they were younger. And sometimes when they were older, depending on the mood.

Isla crossed one leg over the other, clasping her hands over her lap and adjusting the black lace hem of her skirt. She didn't want to think about that today.

Ignoring the guilt that lined the pit of her stomach, she resumed her scan of the audience, and that's when she saw the first living member of her old friend group.

Her heartbeat sped tenfold as Wren Jenkins tossed her long, honey-blonde hair behind her shoulder before dabbing her eyes with a napkin and then letting her hand fall to her stomach. Isla watched Wren make circles around the bump, and her chest tightened. Everything had always come so naturally for Wren. Marriage, motherhood, health, wellness. Hell, even now, Wren's body looked immaculate, even after four kids and another on the way. She was like a golden fertility goddess, a stark contrast to Isla's childless loins and dark, gothic appearance. She'd always felt incomparable to Mother Hen Wren.

Envy started to creep up her vertebrae, one by one, but before the feeling could settle too deeply, she felt a sweep of cool air move by. Stiffening against the rough grain of the pew, Isla turned to the side, heart palpitating like a racehorse. This wasn't the time or the—

"I can't believe you're wearing a hat inside a church."

Liam.

Isla's shoulders relaxed at the sound of his voice.

"I didn't think you were going to be here," she whispered, tipping her black straw hat to the side so she could hug her favorite member of their former clique. "You said you'd be in New York until the end of the month."

Liam pulled away and settled into the pew beside her. "Change of plans. There was no way I was going to miss this."

Isla smiled at his response, a lightness she didn't know she needed pulling inside of her chest; she'd missed him more than she realized. Liam, Rebecca, and Isla were the tightest-knit trio in their group after the pair had absorbed Isla into their world. Liam and Rebecca were the type of people who just paired naturally based on chemistry, an instant connection that only true best friends could share as they delighted in each other's orbit. Isla, on the other hand, had simply been a speckle of lone stardust, floating near their trajectory until gravity sucked her into their path.

If only they'd stayed the course and not burned out, yearning for the brightness of the sun, the complexity of the stars around them, then maybe Rebecca would still be alive.

"Have you seen the others yet?"

Isla startled at Liam's voice again, and she straightened in her seat. "Wren's up there." She paused to nod at the line and waited for Liam's gaze to follow. "I don't know about Scarlett or Carley."

Liam huffed out a laugh. "Oh, you know Scar is never far behind Wren. Those two are still attached at the hip."

Isla smirked, knowing he was right. Scarlett and Wren were another duo the universe could never seem to tear apart. Their bond was stronger than gravity, constantly pulling them back together. Isla used to find it odd that someone as loving and nurturing as Wren gravitated toward a person like Scarlett, an artificial queen bee, but over the years, she realized Wren was just as devious. She was just better at hiding it.

"I saw Carley was in Paraguay last week," Isla whispered, shifting her thoughts. She pulled out her phone to check their other friend's Instagram account, where she was once again startled at the thirty-six-million-count following. No one expected Carley's camping vlog to take off the way it did after she dropped out of college junior year. Isla and the rest of their crew were nasty, cruel even, the way they made fun of her behind her back. Joke's on them now, though, Isla supposed, as Carley was the one living the dream. "If she's off the grid, she may not even know about Bec."

Liam nodded, his gaze drifting back to the line.

"Have you been up there, to see her?" Isla asked after a beat of silence.

He shook his head. "No. Don't want to remember her that way." He paused, raking his fingers through his ashy brown hair, dismantling the carefully gelled spikes. "I'm not good with death, not since—"

Isla's heart squeezed as Liam's voice trailed off, tears forming around his golden irises. It'd been almost two years since Liam lost his little brother, Trey, in a tragic car accident. Since then, he'd been coping by burying his head in the sand and working ridiculous hours at his start-up firm in New York City. He seldom talked about Trey, and Isla was ashamed to admit she sometimes forgot Liam even had a brother.

Another ghost of their past, ready and willing to haunt them.

Just like Rebecca will.

Isla shifted in her seat again, shaking away the thought and giving Liam's hand a light squeeze. "It's okay," she said. "Bec would understand."

Isla felt a small tug back, and then the hum of an old, familiar hymn began buzzing from the front. Suddenly, the crowd caught a rift, a harmonious acapella version of "I'll Fly Away" humming through the air and echoing down the church corridor as everyone sang.

Fly away, Rebecca, Isla thought between each verse. *Fly away from this forsaken place.*

9

SCARLETT
Now

Did Rebecca really have this many friends?

This was the question Scarlett chewed on throughout the entire service. Sure, many people were probably there out of obligation like she was, but it seemed like an awfully big crowd for Rebecca Anders. Not that size mattered, but Scarlett was impressed by how many people her friend's death drew in. Maybe Becca had gotten a leg up in life after all.

She trailed her gaze back to the front where Rebecca's mom and a man she'd never seen before stood in the receiving line. Becca had never talked about her family much after her grandparents passed, and now, Scarlett could see why. Even from a distance, it was obvious her mother was drunk, or high. Or maybe both. Her eyes drooped lower with each blink, and her face was nearly slack-jawed. Some people would say it was just the grief, but Scarlett recognized a junkie when she saw one. She had her father to thank for that.

A cramp unfurled in her stomach then, a double reminder of her own issues. She clutched her stomach, making every attempt to school her features as she outwaited the pain. It had been approximately seventy-two hours since—

No.

Scarlett grimaced, the memory instantly suffocating her.

Deciding she'd made her appearance long enough, Scarlett slid to the end of her pew and tried to make her body smaller than it already was as she ducked out. Once outside, the piercing evening air hit her like a lightning bolt, shocking her senses in the best way. It was early November, and for once, Mother Nature was in alignment with the calendared seasons people so desperately craved. Scarlett took a few more laboring breaths and then stepped onto the pavement, surveying her surroundings.

Various beaten-down Victorian homes lined the walkway, punctuated by the decaying autumnal trees scattered throughout the yards. She rolled her eyes at their lack of gardening and turned back to the street where the city had scattered warm twinkle lights and pine wreaths with red bows across each lamppost, creating the facade of holiday cheer. Wilderby may have been a small town, but it most certainly lacked small-town charm.

The large bell tower above the church tolled, pulling Scarlett's attention away from the lackluster scene, and she counted the chimes, not realizing it was already six o'clock. The time change hadn't happened yet, and she could still feel the last remnants of dusk holding on.

Ready to get the hell out of here and drown her sorrows with a bottle of merlot and a new crime thriller, she pulled out her phone to call her husband, Calvin. He'd refused to come, and honestly, Scarlett didn't blame him. While it was embarrassing for her to be at this event alone, she understood that he didn't want to be in the tabloids. Nothing like sensationalizing a state senator's visit to a podunk girl's funeral.

"Isla! Liam!"

Scarlett turned around at the sound of a familiar, *cringe-worthy* voice, seeing none other than Carley Brunner racing toward Isla Mae Ellis and Liam Walsh. She watched as Carley's pink and brown dreads bounced on top of her head in a lopsided bun. Curious, Scarlett locked her phone and slipped it back into her purse. She hadn't seen the three of them in person since college.

"Well, what do you know?" Liam's distinct voice floated through the fading twilight. "Little Miss Traveling the Globe found her way back to us."

Scarlett watched as Carley's face broke out in a wide, incandescent grin before pulling them both into a hug, and she felt something tug inside her chest. She'd never understood their natural affection toward one another, toward everyone really, except her. Wren was the only one in their friend group who truly cared for Scarlett, and she knew that—was okay with it, mostly. But Scar would be lying if she said she didn't envy the instant connection the others felt.

A lone two seconds of pity settled beneath the surface of her skin before she shed it, replacing it with new, stronger cells. Then, she decided to join them.

"It's West Virginia, honey," she heard Liam say as she approached. "What'd you expect?"

Of course Carley's complaining about the weather.

Scarlett rolled her eyes as her heels clicked against the pavement. "Carley Brunner, I do declare!" She did her best to draw out her Southern accent, a charm her mother had long ago taught her.

Immediately, three sets of eyes were on her, but no one spoke.

Scarlett felt the weight of her intimidation and tried again. "What are you doing in this neck of the woods?"

"Scarlett," Carley finally said after a hesitant beat. "How are you?"

"How am I?" Scar feigned a gasp, placing a hand on her chest before lightly tapping Carley's. "How are you? Always traipsing off this way and that, making a living through the mud and dirt."

She hadn't meant it to come out as an insult, but Scarlett preferred to call a spade a spade.

"Oh, you know me," Carley answered, not even batting an eye. "Just living my dream life—making a difference in the world. How about you, Scar? How does it feel to be married to a senator now? You must love being his arm candy at events."

Scarlett's jaw clenched. Everyone knew it was her dream to be in politics, to be the next Hilary Clinton and fight for equality and women's rights. But, after learning how difficult it was to make it in this world as a female, and how much easier it was when linked to a man, well, she'd since been *domesticated* for the time being. She told herself it would all be worth it in the end.

"It is just darling getting to serve at his right-hand side," she finally said after recovering her face. "Maybe you'd like to tag along for our holiday fundraiser next weekend. I can introduce you to somebody, maybe help you find a man to finally settle down with."

And there it was, the universe whispered.

The transference of power was restored, yet again.

"Scar, be nice," another familiar voice said from behind. "Not everybody wants to be tied down and married with babies."

Scarlett's eyebrow twitched as Wren came into view.

"Hey, friends," Wren said, immediately wrapping her arm around Carley's neck, then Liam's and Isla's at the same time. "Long time no see."

Liam spoke next, placing his hands on her belly without warning. He always did have boundary issues. "Girl, is this baby number five? I should've had you be our surrogate instead of that woman Ben knows." He paused, lowering his voice so the baby wouldn't hear. "She was an *ass*."

Wren chuckled and twisted the end of one of her blonde curls, leaving Scarlett once again envious of her next statement. "It's funny you should say that. This actually isn't my baby."

13

Isla responded this time, her pale face twisted into something unreadable. "You mean . . ."

Wren nodded. "Yes, this little love bug is a surro-baby, a sweet little girl. I figured it was about time I started popping out kids for women who can't have babies themselves. It's so rewarding, knowing I can give someone else the gift of life and then go home to sleep at night."

Ugh.

Isla muttered something under her breath, and Scarlett couldn't handle it anymore. She needed air, time, space. Anything to put distance between her and this constant reminder of her failure.

On the flip side, she also wasn't ready to be alone. As much as she hated to admit it, she needed someone right now. She needed a friend.

"Well, I, for one, could use a drink." She quickly scanned the group, hoping her tone would steer them toward a new topic. "Thick Chicks, anyone?"

The invitation felt forced, and she knew it, but maybe this would be good. A chance for them to all reconnect, see her in a better light.

Scarlett felt a hand grip her shoulder as Wren leaned on her for support, slipping her shoes off. "I could definitely use a mocktail. My feet are killing me, and I cannot go home to those children yet. This is the first night Brennan's been home alone with them in weeks—let's take advantage of it."

"A husband who's home. What a nice thought," Scarlett mumbled, her voice barely audible.

WREN
Now

MOMENTS LATER, THE GROUP filled into a large round booth at the old university pub, and Wren felt an odd sense of comfort. The five of them hadn't been together like this since their junior year at Ridge Haven University when they sent Carley off for her first backpacking trip. That was almost a decade ago, and suddenly, she couldn't believe how much time had passed.

Sure, she saw Scar regularly, but Scar was . . . well, Wren could only handle so much of her at once. She loved the woman but was often left feeling mentally drained after their conversations. Point being, it was a nice change of pace to have everyone back together again.

The only one missing was Becca.

Not wanting to cry again, Wren distracted herself with the menu, but it wasn't long before the baby she was carrying decided to bury itself into her bladder.

Sighing, she slammed the laminated paper down. "I have to pee again. I'll be right back."

"Say hi to Isla while you're in there." Liam spoke in a nonchalant manner, but the comment struck Wren as odd. She didn't even see Isla leave the table.

Chalking it up to pregnancy brain, Wren waddled off to the bathroom, trying her damndest not to let any pee sprinkle out in the process. But when she pushed the door open, she heard a faint cry, surprising her and sending a small dribble down her leg.

"Dammit," she said under her breath before waddling farther in.

Another minuscule sob sounded from behind one of the stalls, yet again capturing her attention. It sounded like—

"Isla?"

Wren's voice echoed in the bathroom, and for a moment, it was silent. She had heard a noise, right?

In the quiet, someone hiccuped, confirming her suspicions.

"Yeah?"

That was definitely Isla.

Still barefoot save for the tights, Wren padded against the cool, tiled floor until she stood outside the handicap stall. "Are you okay, hun?"

She heard her friend clearing her throat before a mere "Mhm" echoed under the door. Wren chewed her bottom lip for a moment, not sure what to do. Crying wasn't exactly *on brand* for Isla—the woman rarely showed human emotion—but they had just said goodbye to one of their oldest friends. Maybe she needed a shoulder to cry on, just this once.

Wren took a deep breath and shifted her weight from one foot to the next, still painfully aware of her bladder. "Do you wanna talk about it?" A pause, and then she added, "It's just me."

16

Silence met her on the other side of the stall yet again, but then, without warning, Isla undid the lock and slid to the floor, the words spilling out of her at lightning speed. "I thought I was *pregnant*."

Her voice cracked at the confession, and the words hit Wren like a supernova. Suddenly, she didn't have to pee anymore.

"I thought it worked," Isla continued, nearly choking on her words as she clasped her arms around her stomach. "I had blood work this morning, and I—just thought—for sure—that the IVF worked this time."

"Oh, honey," Wren said, rushing to her friend's side and recovering her facial features from the initial shock. "Honey, I'm so sorry." She wrapped her arms around Isla's shaking frame, doing her best not to let her bump get in the way as the irony of the situation was not lost on her.

Isla sniffled, continuing to cry. "David doesn't even know. He gave me custody of our last embryo, thinking I would donate it when I was mentally ready, but I used it instead without telling him."

Oh, boy, Wren thought. *Here we go.*

"And, and I really thought, *this is it. This is how you're going to get pregnant, Isla*. And I was okay with being a single mom as long as I had my baby."

Wren chewed her lip, waiting for more.

"I got the call from my doctor on the drive down here, but I was hoping they were wrong, that maybe we'd just scheduled the blood draw too early, but then I came in here to pee, and the damn toilet paper had blood on it, and I just—"

Isla burst into another sob, clinging to Wren's chest as she sat there, bewildered.

She had no idea the amount of information overload she was stepping into.

"There, there," she said after a moment, rubbing circles on Isla's back.

Then, she started to say it was all going to be okay but clamped her mouth shut, thinking better of it. Wren had never lost a child before, but she imagined it to be the most horrendous thing any woman or parent could go through. She also had no idea what it felt like to struggle to conceive. She and Brennan

17

had gotten pregnant without even trying for their first kid, and honestly, the rest of them were barely planned before the pregnancy tests started popping up positive. It was part of the reason why she'd agreed to be a surrogate—to help other women in need.

And now, here she was, holding her dear friend who had a failed IVF transfer, while she sat seven months pregnant with someone else's baby. The situation almost made her feel guilty for how many healthy, living children she had.

"I'm so sorry," Wren cooed again, hugging her friend closer. "I know how much you wanted this."

Her words fell flat, but she didn't know what else to say.

"I just don't understand," Isla finally mumbled after a few minutes had passed. "It's so easy for you, and so many others. Why can't I have a baby in my belly?"

Her voice was smaller now, and Wren held her tighter, wishing she knew what to say. Despite her nickname, she had no idea how to "mother hen" Isla out of this situation. It was delicate, and given her current state, she didn't believe she was the right person for this conversation. So, instead of talking, Wren simply held Isla, catching her tears in the soft fabric of her maternity dress as they fell.

Eventually, Wren knew the others would start to worry, and she could only assume the last thing Isla wanted was for them to know, especially Scarlett. Isla had always been private, and Wren knew the only reason she had confided in her was because she was in the right place at the right time.

So, to save her friend the embarrassment, she said, "Oh, I'm just so sorry, honey. Do you want me to tell the others you had to leave?"

Isla seemed to understand and pulled away quickly, wiping her face. "No." She shook her head. "No, I'll be fine. I'm sorry; I didn't mean to dump that on you."

Wren offered a small smile, the corners of her nude-colored lips turning upright. "You don't have to apologize to me, hun. I just wish there was something I could do to help."

An involuntary laugh escaped Isla's mouth. "There's nothing anyone can do, unless you wanna give me that baby instead of those other people."

Wren knew it was a joke, but the way Isla said it sent a chill down her spine. "Oh," she started, trying to erase the feeling. "You know I would carry your baby any day, girl. You just say the word."

Isla nodded, wiping her cheeks and blinking rapidly several times as she attempted to stave off the tears.

"Come on," Wren said decidedly, waddling her way back into a standing position. "Let's go get you a drink." Her surro-baby kicked again, this time slamming straight into her bladder. "Actually, hold that thought. I never peed."

This forced a light, genuine laugh out of Isla.

When Wren was finished and had washed her hands, the two linked arms, ready to return to the group.

Just as Wren began to open the door, Isla stopped dead in her tracks. "Hey, please don't—"

"Say anything to the others," Wren finished for her. She could always read Isla like a book. "Wouldn't dream of it."

She winked at her friend and started counting down the minutes until she could waddle home and tell Brennan everything.

She had to tell *somebody* the tea.

LIAM

NOW

LIAM FELT THE WARM buzz of his drink humming in his body.

He *hated* funerals, probably more than most people. But that's likely par for the course when you've experienced as much loss as he had. First, his mom, then his grandmother, and then Trey. It seemed like no matter how good he was or how well life treated him, everyone he loved eventually died, like instead of a black thumb, he harbored the black plague.

And now here he was, tending to yet another loss with a group of women he half-hated, half-loved.

Cue sad-boy era.

"Isla!" Carley nearly screamed, pulling Liam from his thoughts. He noted a subtle new tone in her dialect and smiled, wondering which country she'd picked that up from. She used to have a hick accent like the rest of them, but little by little, he noticed the subtle changes with each new video she posted, like she was collecting all her favorite pieces of the world in her voice, creating a unique sound that was all her own. "Please tell me you remember the time your mom took Rebecca and us to TP her ex-boyfriend's house in middle school."

Liam kicked back the rest of his beer as the others reminisced. He'd heard this story a million times, but the nostalgia of it all brought him comfort, nonetheless.

"Yeah," Isla said, dipping another pita chip in the buffalo dip they'd ordered. "Jeremiah Lane. Couldn't stand that guy."

Carley nodded, stifling a laugh. "Your mom parked in the alley behind the street, and we all dressed in black and had hoodies and everything."

"Yeah, and freaking Rebecca bombed his windows with eggs, and he woke up," Isla said.

Liam smirked. "Classic Bec. I still can't believe your mom took you guys to do that."

Isla flashed a genuine smile, revealing faded spots where her dark lipstick had flaked off. "Yeah, my mom was fun growing up."

"Can't say the same for Rebecca's mom," Carley said, a loose dread falling from her bun. "Can you imagine if she knew half the shit we did?" She paused to take a sip of her drink, some foreign concoction she'd convinced the bartender to make for her. "She would've locked her up and thrown away the key."

"Oh my gosh, remember that time she followed you guys home from the movies?" Wren asked, her eyes wide.

"Mhm," Liam and Isla answered in unison. Then Isla added, "That was not a fun night."

Scarlett tilted her head and spoke for the first time. "I don't remember that."

Shocker, Liam thought.

He glanced at the others before Wren piped up, saving the day. "I think you were prepping for the SATs. We told Rebecca's mom we were going to the movies alone, but it was really so she could see Henry Lloyd. Turns out, Mrs.

Anders had followed us there and the whole drive home. She ripped Rebecca a new one after that."

The waitress returned to drop off another round of drinks, and a heartbreaking sense of déjà vu overcame him. How many times had he been here, sitting in this exact spot while Becca waited on them? Dropping off drinks at their table. Stealing fries as soon as she delivered their food. Living her best life despite it all.

"I still can't believe she's gone." His voice was low, catching the others off guard with the sudden shift in tone.

Nobody spoke for a moment, and he stared at the bead of sweat forming on the outside of his glass, wondering what it must have felt like, to have known she was taking her last breath. He didn't know much about anatomy or physiology, but he imagined her death wasn't a speedy process. Not like people who die instantly, like his mom and brother had. Hell, even his grandma was fortunate enough to pass away in her sleep, meaning she never knew it was happening.

But Rebecca, she must've felt it, sensed it as she lay there on the floor, waiting for someone who would never come to her rescue. She must've mentally grasped what was happening, yet was physically incapable of stopping it.

He shuddered at the thought and took another swig of his drink, savoring the amber burn as it dulled his pain.

So much for drinking to forget.

SEVERAL DRINKS—AND STORIES—LATER, EVERYONE but Wren was drunk, successfully drowning their sorrows in booze.

"All right," Carley slurred, clinking her half-full glass against Liam's half-empty one. "Southern Belle or Fireball shots?"

He immediately recoiled, memories of their youth flooding back. "Isn't part of being an adult not having to drink shitty alcohol anymore?" Besides, this beer was getting the job done rather effectively. Liam was safely in the do-not-drive zone.

"Come on, Liam!" Carley slurred again, her inner lush coming out.

He started to roll his eyes and turn her down, but Isla spoke up before he could, raising her black coffin nails in the air and twirling her fingers. "Why not both?"

That elicited a laugh from Scarlett. "Isla Mae, are you trying to make us puke?" Her twang was even more exaggerated, thanks to the magical number of cocktails that kept appearing at her side.

"What?" Isla rebutted. "Don't feel like doing the old puke and rally, Scar? Come on, I didn't take you for a quitter. Where's your sense of spirit?"

Liam felt the weight of Isla's challenge as soon as the words hit the air, and he was instantly transported back to high school, where he often sat sidelined while Scar and Isla had it out. He could never pinpoint why exactly, but the two had more animosity between them than anyone else in the group. Not that he was blaming Isla—everyone disliked Scarlett to a degree. She was naturally bitchy and unapologetic about it. But what really puzzled him was why Scarlett picked on Isla more than anyone else.

Jealousy, perhaps.

Insecurity was the root of all high school drama, wasn't it? The true making of any mean girl.

Or mean guy, in his case.

"Actually, you know what?" Scarlett pushed a loose strand of icy blonde hair out of her face and slid a finger into the air, signaling the waitress. "One round of Southern Belles and Fireball shots on me, please and thank you."

Liam raised one of his carefully threaded brows and let out a breath he absolutely knew he was holding. "Y'all are paying for my Uber tonight."

Wren chimed in at that, talking around the fry in her mouth. "Don't worry, hun. I'll drive y'all home tonight. Lord knows I've got the space. Ain't nothing mini about a minivan."

23

Although hesitant, Liam accepted the free drinks when they arrived, and as they trickled down his windpipe and into his bloodstream, he felt his earlier, more rigid thoughts melting away.

The others must have also felt the effects because, subtly, the snide remarks began to halt. And in place of them were more fond memories from their childhood, all the way up until they went their separate ways in college.

"Would you look at this," Carley said, slinging an arm around Isla. "The Fire Tribe is back together again, y'all. I love it!"

"Fire Tribe?" Scarlett said in a high-pitched tone, at first mocking their old nickname but then surprising everyone with her next statement. "I want to see the Everclear Kids back in action."

The group audibly groaned.

"I can't believe we used to drink that stuff." Liam scrubbed a hand over his face, feeling a mix of exhaustion and excitement. "I'll never get over how little, tiny Becca tipped back the jug and drank it straight without a chaser or anything."

"Yeah, and then she fucking dropped it like it was a damn microphone." Carley snorted, slurping the last of her water.

Liam smiled at the memory, wishing he could have one last drink with his oldest friend.

Rebecca would like this, he thought.

And then he said it out loud.

Everyone turned to him, but he didn't feel the need to elaborate. Despite all the bullshit he and these women had endured throughout those cruel, pre-pubescent years, an unspoken comfort was woven between them. Sure, they'd made up mean rumors about each other, stolen a boyfriend or two, and there was that awful incident with Quinn Waterbury, but those experiences were what ultimately connected them.

They knew each other's truest selves, their meanest parts, and yet, they still accepted one another. They'd grown up and moved on, forgiving each other of their past transgressions.

As odd as it may seem, there was something to be said about people you could be your absolute worst self with.

Or at least, that's what Liam thought.

"You know," Wren said, removing her palms from her growing belly and placing them on the table instead. "I think Rebecca would want us to do something to remember her by. Like, more than this." She made a wide circle with her arm, motioning to the group.

Liam scrunched his nose, confusion shooting into the divets of his early onset wrinkles—a genetic trait he most definitely blamed his father for. "What do you mean?"

"I mean," Wren said, grabbing another handful of fries. "Rebecca would've wanted us all together again. Would've wanted us to celebrate her life beyond just this one night."

"What did you have in mind?" Isla asked, puckering her lips as she sucked on a lemon, a vibrant contrast against her dark lipstick.

But Wren didn't answer right away. Instead, she nibbled at her food as the rest of the group sat, silent in thought. Liam thought back to all the memorials he'd been to for his family members, instantly knowing he didn't want to attend anymore. Plus, Rebecca wouldn't have wanted a candlelight vigil or a fundraiser walk or anything stupid like that. If they were going to do something in honor of her memory, it needed to be fun, spontaneous, and carefree. Something that represented her.

He scratched the back of his neck, willing his brain to function through the wave of intoxication clouding his thoughts. It was on the tip of his tongue, almost there, floating in the recesses of his mind, yet he couldn't put it into words.

Then suddenly, Wren squealed, the answer clicking into place in a slow, steady haze. "I've got it," she said, nearly knocking over her mocktail.

Liam swung his head back in her direction as he attempted to swallow a burp.

"What if," Wren started, pausing for what Liam could only assume was dramatic effect, "we did Secret Santa again?"

REBECCA

THEN

MAGICAL.

Tonight was going to be magical; Rebecca could feel it.

It was the evening of her friends' annual Secret Santa tradition, and she was determined to make it their best one yet. Rebecca loved the holidays, more than any of them, and she had taken on the responsibility of ensuring each year was better than the last. What had started as a one-time thing during their freshman year of high school quickly morphed into something else, eliciting an electric bond between her and her friends.

She washed her toothbrush off and smiled at her reflection, remembering how she'd sat down with Isla, Liam, Wren, Scarlett, and Carley to discuss their plans last year during their first semester at RHU. She had initially worried the tradition would fizzle out after high school, but to her surprise, everyone who'd kept in touch still wanted to move forward. Rebecca practically glowed when they accepted her offer to host a sleepover after the dinner party, complete with spiked hot chocolate, red and green Jell-O shots, and her grandma's famous sugar cookies—God rest her soul.

The night had been such a hit that Rebecca suggested they draw names earlier this year, and no one objected as they dove head-first into another busy semester of classes. Becca drew first that day, and although she felt a hint of disappointment when she saw Scarlett's name, she was still elated. Sure, she had to pick up extra shifts at Thick Chicks to foot the bill, but it was worth it.

They were all worth it.

Her Christmas playlist shuffled to the next song in the background, and she splashed water on her face, singing along to "Deck da Club" by the Ying Yang Twins as she finished her mental checklist.

Tonight, they would be dining at Bella Cucina's, Wilderby's nicest Italian restaurant, and afterward, they would stay at Scarlett's townhouse for their sleepover. Becca had spent weeks searching for the ideal pair of Christmas PJs and thrifting for vintage Santa mugs to surprise everyone with, and she'd be damned if this wasn't going to be the most magical night for her and her friends yet.

After generously applying makeup, curling her hair, and changing into the emerald dress she'd been hoarding since last year's day-after-Christmas sale, Rebecca stood in front of the full-length mirror in her living room, admiring her appearance. She was normally self-conscious, more so than most women, but tonight, she felt beautiful. Her red locks fell in waves over her creamy skin, the perfect contrast to the jewel tone of her cocktail dress. The cut was form-fitting in a way that accentuated what little curves she did have without drawing attention to her small pooch. Rebecca had tried desperately throughout the years to get rid of it, but no matter how many meals she skipped or how much she threw up, the skin refused to move.

Smoothing the gown over her hips, she darted her eyes up, meeting her own gaze. Tonight, she reminded herself, was about joy. She would laugh with her friends, drink without remorse, and *eat* good food. She would not think about the number of calories consumed or the extra trans fat in her entrée. She'd even already called the restaurant to ask what ingredients were in her meal of choice. Tonight, she would feel confident. She promised to give her body grace.

"Oh my gosh, I knew it!" Rebecca squealed as Carley handed her a stack of presents from across the table. "I knew you had me." Her body was giddy from the secret finally being revealed.

"You did not," Carley said back, a shocked expression on her face.

Rebecca laughed. "Yes, I totally did. I mean, I didn't *know* know, but like, I knew. You know?" She quickly ripped apart the packaging, anxious to see what her friend had picked out for her. "Oh my gosh, Car!" She nearly screamed as the vinyl record of Taylor Swift's newest album stared back at her. "I've been dying for this. How did you find one? I thought they were sold out."

Carley shrugged. "I know places."

Eyes widening, Rebecca had to stifle another scream as her friend quoted one of the songs from 1989. "This is seriously perfect. Thank you."

"You're welcome! Now go on, open the rest."

Becca obliged, pulling out a Bath and Body Works candle, a cream-colored sweater, and a plastic candy cane full of mini Fireball bottles. It was literally her perfect gift.

"Okay, you two," Liam said, interrupting their happy bubble. "Get on with it so the rest of us can open our gifts. I'm dying over here."

Releasing Carley from a quick hug, Rebecca returned to her seat and started pulling out her gifts. "Okaaaaay," she said, drawing out the suspense. "I haaaaaad . . . Scarlett!"

"Dammit," Liam said at the same time Scarlett let out a shocked breath. "I definitely thought you had me this year."

"So did I," Isla said, scowling. "You were so secretive. I thought for sure it was because you had me."

Rebecca felt a sense of pride at surprising everyone. She was usually the worst with secrets, especially when it came to this. It usually went without fail that everyone knew who she had within a week of drawing names.

"I promised myself I would actually keep it a secret this year." She shrugged, handing the last of her bags to Scarlett.

What she didn't share was the only reason she'd accomplished this was because of her therapist. The university provided free therapy through the psychology department, and her counselor had really been helping Rebecca see the value in herself and shifting her perspective on a lot of things. She told her it was important to not break promises to herself, the same way she wouldn't for a friend. Becca assumed this was a good place to start.

But she wasn't ready to share that detail yet. Although Bec loved her friends, she also knew how deep their gossip mill ran. She didn't feel like giving them another reason to make fun of her, to think less of her. They all knew her family drama—a deadbeat father, a strung-out mother, and a loving set of grandparents who'd passed long ago. They didn't need another reminder of where she came from. Especially when she'd finally gained a higher spot in their good graces.

Taking a quick sip of water, she looked at Scarlett and watched her tear at the tissue paper before pulling out her main gift. Rebecca had spent several of her paychecks and all her spare tips from Thick Chicks to pay for it, but it was worth it when she saw the surprised yet satisfied look on Scarlett's face.

"I love it," Scar said, her genuine smile beaming as she admired the Michael Kors purse. "Thank you so much, Bec."

The gratification was like an instant hit of morphine to Rebecca's soul. She loosed a breath and smiled in return. "I'm so glad to hear you say that."

ISLA

NOW

"SECRET SANTA?" ISLA SAT up, straightening her spine and sucking in her bottom lip as her eyes widened. "Seriously?"

"Yeah, why not?" Wren countered, her eyes twinkling like a fairy godmother. "I mean, think about it. Which one of us loved our Secret Santa tradition more than anybody?"

Isla chanced a glance at Liam, then Carley, then Scar.

They didn't have to say her name. They already knew the answer.

Rebecca.

Rebecca had adored their holiday tradition. While everyone else was glad to participate, Rebecca was always the driving force, reminding them all of what was to come and using cliché phrases like "the magic of Christmas." She would show up to class in ugly Christmas sweaters the entire week leading up to the exchange, and she was always the first to organize wish lists and reservations. Then, as everyone got older, she started putting together an after-party, which for the two years it happened before everyone drifted apart, was an old-fashioned slumber party—grown-up edition. She'd insisted everyone wear Christmas pajamas and then would surprise the group with homemade sugar cookies and extra goodies.

It was the highlight of her year, and likely everyone else's, if Isla was being honest.

Too bad it wasn't enough to hide the crack in her illusion.

"I think it could be fun," Scarlett said, surprising Isla. "It would be nice to have something nonpolitical to look forward to during the holidays."

Wren squealed, rubbing her stomach and causing Isla to wince at the phantom feeling in her own belly. "See, it's perfect!"

Isla sat back, playing with the black hem of her dress. It's not that she didn't want to do it; it sounded fun, great actually. The thought of partaking in another year of Secret Santa with her oldest friends sparked a constellation of hope and joy in her chest. It had been nearly a decade since the tradition abruptly ended, and the idea of rekindling it in Bec's honor was almost enough to make her forget the pain in her chest.

But if she was being honest with herself—and she was, Scout's honor—the idea also frightened her for reasons she couldn't, wouldn't address.

"I don't know," she said after a pregnant pause. "I'm going to be playing catch-up at work for the next week after missing the past few days. Plus, the assistant manager I hired still isn't fully trained. I really can't take any more time off work." Her little coffee shop may not be at the franchise level, but it was doing well. She stayed afloat and lived a comfortable life, much to her ex-husband's dismay. He would've loved to see her fail.

"Seriously, Isla?" Scarlett raised an annoyed brow. "You, of all people, should be able to get away more than anyone. You're the owner of that damn coffee shop, for Heaven's sake. What's the point of owning a business if you can't let the people you hire run it for you?"

Said the woman who's clearly never owned a business a day in her life.

"It doesn't really work like that."

"I don't know, Isla," Carley said, puckering her lips after one too many lemon drops. "I actually think Scar has a point. It would be so much fun to get everyone together again, away from all the death and despair. And really, it'd only be one night. Surely you can sneak away for a quick weekend trip."

Feeling the defeat rattle in her bones, Isla looked to Liam for salvation. "What about you? I'm sure you're too busy to get away."

He answered with a shrug. "The firm is closed the whole week of Christmas. As long as everyone is good with doing it the Saturday before so I could be home in time to celebrate with Ben and the twins, then sure. I don't see why not."

That wasn't the answer she was hoping for. Isla looked away and snatched the latest shot of Fireball off the table. Tossing her head back, she savored the room-temperature burn on the way down. Once in college, she'd tried a chilled cinnamon shot at one of the local bars and had almost thrown up. It wasn't until later she realized the liquid's temperature was what threw her off.

Now, as the spicy whiskey trickled down her sternum and into her belly, she couldn't help but notice the warmth blooming in her chest. The idea of returning to Wilderby again, honoring their dead friend's memory somewhere other than a dingy bar pub, while having the attention of the people she'd so desperately sought approval from all those years ago, made her feel lighter.

Enticed.

Maybe she could do this . . .

She watched now as Wren adjusted herself in her chair, clearly uncomfortable, and that's when Isla's reality came crashing back down in a startling wave.

"I can't," she said, the words spilling out faster than the lie could form. "I forgot I have to get my wisdom teeth cut out that day."

Scarlett scrunched her face in horror, her hazel eyes more piercing than stalactites. "You have oral surgery on a Saturday? The Saturday before Christmas?"

Isla nodded. "Mhm. Yep. The doctor came highly recommended, and I've been on his waitlist for a cancellation for months." She paused to shake a few pieces of ice into her mouth, crunching on the half-frozen cubes in an attempt to ground herself. How many drinks did she have again? "Sorry, y'all, but I'll have to pass."

"Isla Mae Ellis, don't you know my husband is the best dentist in this whole county?" Isla snapped her head back to Wren, surprised by her tone of voice. "He can fix your teeth tonight if you want." A pause and then, "Well, on second thought, you've had a lot of alcohol, so not tonight, but you get the point."

"Oh, come on, y'all." Carley was beaming now, one pink dreaded tendril framing her face. "Let's do it. I think it's a great idea."

Isla started to object again, but Liam cut her off. "Ah, fuck it." Then he threw back another beer and added, "Why the hell not? I'm in."

Her jaw dropped open at his words, and she was too drunk to remind herself to close it.

"But, but," Isla stammered, desperately trying to think of another excuse, one that would make sense without giving herself away.

But her efforts were useless. Scarlett's blinding rays began clouding her vision as the weight of Scar's gravitational pull reeled her in.

"Come on, Isla," she said, brushing a hair out of her face with a carefully manicured nail. "Don't be such a Grinch. We should do this, for Rebecca."

Since when did Scarlett care about Rebecca?

The question hit her like a meteor shower, striking in various places all at once. Scarlett was always the first to make fun of Rebecca when they were younger, both to her face and behind her back. She'd made it known on more than one occasion her distaste for their friend, but for whatever reason, Becca had never minded, was oblivious to it even. Isla had always thought it was sad.

She opened her mouth to voice these opinions, deciding now was as good a time as any to air out their grievances, but before she had a chance, Carley slammed her camera bag on the center of the table.

"Here," Car said. "We can draw names out of this. Let me just get my camera out."

"I have paper!" Wren chimed, a sing-song edge to her voice.

Isla's mind swirled as the copious amounts of alcohol caught up with her. "Wait—" she tried, and failed, to get their attention. To say no before everyone found out her secret.

But no one was listening.

Instead, four hands were busy pulling out small pieces of scrap paper until there was only one left.

"Here, Isla." Liam nudged her this time, scooting the bag closer to her. "Last one's for you."

With all eyes on her and the act already in motion, she realized she had no choice but to participate.

"Fine," she mumbled under her breath before sitting up and dipping her hand into the black canvas bag. Her fingers wrapped around the small piece of paper, and before she knew it, she was staring down at eight little letters scribbled in red.

Scarlett.

REBECCA
THEN

"Y'ALL READY?" REBECCA CALLED over her shoulder as she put the final touches on her green lipstick.

She and her friends were heading to the Kappa house for their annual St. Patrick's Day party, and Rebecca was ecstatic to be off work. She always had to work during holidays and fun events since starting at Thick Chicks, but by the grace of God, she'd somehow scored tonight off.

"Hold on." Isla came into view from her room. They'd been sharing an apartment together since the start of the spring semester, and Rebecca had to admit, it had its perks.

Isla spun around now, showing off her lace black romper. "Okay, how do I look?"

Rebecca raised a brow. "You know you're supposed to wear green today, right?"

"Yeah, I know." Isla looked down at her outfit, double-checking the length as she bent over. "There," she said, standing back up.

Satisfied with her own appearance, Becca turned around to see what Isla was talking about.

When she saw it, she laughed. "A shamrock necklace. Really? Where's your sense of spirit? Your holiday pride!"

"David likes this outfit," she said simply. "I want to wear it for him."

Rebecca smirked at her friend. "Y'all are gross."

Isla laughed, but Becca was serious. Since moving in together, Isla's boyfriend, David, was over at their place at least three or four nights a week. Rebecca didn't totally mind, especially since he bought them food regularly and always put the seat down in the bathroom—unlike her ex—but the two were so wrapped up around each other that it made all the single people in the room—i.e. Rebecca—super uncomfortable.

"You're just jealous." Isla shrugged on a coat and grabbed her phone from the counter while Rebecca sighed.

"I guess you're right. I want someone to be sickeningly sweet with me again."

It'd been nearly six months since she broke up with her loser ex-boyfriend for cheating on her, and she'd been in a dry spell ever since.

"The right person will come along when you least expect it," Isla said, brushing past her and opening the door. "That's what happened to me with David. You just gotta stop focusing on finding the right person and instead, focus on becoming the right person. That's all you can do, babe."

Becca met her friend's gaze and then quickly looked down, embarrassed by the sudden tears that threatened her lash line. "Dammit, Isla, I worked hard on this makeup!" She let out a nervous laugh and then shook out her amber curls, recovering from the faulty emotion quickly.

"Come on. Let's go drink it off and have some fun."

Twenty minutes later, Rebecca followed Isla inside the Kappa Sigma house, the smell of beer and body odor already wafting through the air.

She pinched the bridge of her nose, momentarily second-guessing her decision to come here.

"Hey, there you guys are!"

Exhaling a steady breath, Rebecca looked up in search of the familiar voice and saw David walking toward them.

"I was starting to get worried." He bent down and gave Isla a kiss while Becca glanced away, already blushing from their embrace.

After everyone had exchanged greetings and taken off their coats, David led them into the kitchen, where the rest of their friends were already playing beer pong.

Rebecca giggled as she watched Carley bounce a white ball into her opponent's red Solo cup and then scream as she high-fived Liam. "Told you bitches we'd win!"

"Yeah," Liam agreed, cupping his hands over his mouth and yelling over the music. "No one stands a chance against The Dream Team."

Music continued to bump in the background, but Rebecca could clearly see the other two guys' pissed-off faces.

"Y'all are embarrassing," Scarlett said, hopping down from her spot on the counter and turning toward Rebecca, Isla, and David. "David, make yourself useful and fetch your woman and Becca a drink before they die of boredom."

Becca and Isla exchanged a knowing glance. Scar always had such a way with words.

"Yes, ma'am." David threw up his hands in mock defeat, feigning a look of innocence. "Any preference, ladies?"

"No liquor for me!" Becca yelled as Iggy Azalea's new song boomed over the speakers. "Just beer, please."

David waited for Isla to give him her order and then waved a hand, promising to be back soon.

"He's a keeper, Isla." Wren's words came out slurred, and Rebecca wondered how much she'd already had to drink. "You should marry him."

"Please," Scarlett interjected, rolling her eyes. "Not everyone came to school just to get their Mrs. Degree, Wren."

Rebecca tuned out their banter and scanned the crowd, eyeing the men who were there. She didn't notice anyone right off the bat, but the blond guy hanging out by the patio door seemed cute enough. Maybe if she had enough liquid courage, she would go talk to him later.

As if on cue, David reappeared at her side with a green drink in hand. "Green beer for St. Patty's Day. No clue what it actually is. Tastes like piss, though, so my guess is Corona."

Becca snorted, slipping the drink from his hand, suddenly feeling grateful for another man besides Liam she could trust in these situations. "Thank you!"

She took a sip of the drink, unbothered by its marijuana-like taste. In an odd way, it reminded her of home. And in an even weirder way, that provided her with comfort. Something else she'd definitely have to talk to her therapist about.

Liam bumped Bec's shoulder, and she started to tease him about it but stopped when she saw the look on his face. "What's wrong?"

He nodded his head toward the front door. "Look who just walked in."

Becca turned, following his gaze until her eyes landed on a familiar friend.

Or rather, an ex-friend.

Quinn.

"What is *she* doing here?" Scar's holier-than-thou voice trailed from behind Rebecca.

Probably exactly what we are, Bec wanted to say but didn't.

Isla pushed herself off the counter where she'd been nursing a drink. "Do you guys think we should go say hi?"

Wren answered without missing a beat. "Absolutely not. Y'all gotta let that shit go. We tried to make amends with her; she wasn't interested." She stumbled to the nearby trash can, chucking yet another empty seltzer. "Bless and release, y'all. Bless and release."

Becca, Isla, and Liam all exchanged a knowing glance, their silence speaking volumes. Quinn was their friend in high school, one they were all close with in different ways. Unfortunately for her, though, she fell victim to one of their cruelest pranks to date, and although they apologized, the moment they graduated, she never spoke to them again. Becca had approached her once, seeing her on campus during their freshman year at RHU, but Quinn snubbed her.

"Come on!" Carley's voice cut in, distracting everyone before the memory could consume them. "I'm not gonna let Quinn Waterbury ruin our night. She's not worth our time. Let's dance."

Although hesitant, Rebecca let her friend lead her to the dance floor, where they spent several hours shamelessly grinding against one another as the drinks continued to flow.

At one point, Becca became dizzy, making it difficult to stand, when familiar hands caught her fall.

"Davey!" She slurred his name as the room spun. "Dave, I—I don't feel so good."

"It's okay," he said, voice low. "I've got you. Let's go sit down."

Rebecca nodded, thinking that definitely sounded like a good idea. "Where's Isla?"

"She's fine. With the others playing beer pong again."

"Again!" Rebecca screamed and then stumbled over something—or someone. She really wasn't sure at this point. "Our girl loooooooves pongin' it."

She continued to follow David's lead, not realizing until the lighting changed that they weren't downstairs anymore.

"David, where are we?" She spun in a half-circle, squinting her bleary green eyes and trying to place her surroundings.

Fuck, how many drinks did she have?

"Dave—"

His lips cut off her words, and it took her brain way too long to catch up to what was happening.

"Hey!" she finally said, doing her best to shove him off. "What the hell are you doing?"

"Come on, Becca." He gripped her waist, pulling her back toward him. "I see the way you look at me. The way you look at *us* when we're at the apartment. You want me. And that's okay, because I want you, too."

What the hell is happening?

Rebecca didn't *want* him. She would never sleep with her best friend's boyfriend, not in a million years! Sure, she was lonely and envious of what they had, but she would never dishonor the girl code that way.

David's hands were roaming her body, and alarm bells went off at an increasingly fast rate.

"Get off me." She tried to shove him again, but her limbs seemed to have stopped working.

David clearly wasn't listening as he pressed his lips to the nape of her neck, and Rebecca felt her entire body scream under the surface.

Why wasn't he stopping?

And why couldn't she stand?

Rebecca tried pushing him off again, but he quickly gripped her arms and pushed her down. Before she knew it, she was lying on the bed and could feel him tugging her clothes off.

"Please," she begged, each moment harder to function. "Stop."

"Just relax, Bec. You won't remember this in the morning."

Her skin was on fire. Every part of her wanted to crawl in and outside of itself, if only to escape his touch.

But there was nothing she could do.

Hours later, when she was alone and naked and afraid, it was Scarlett who found her.

ISLA
NOW

Two days later, Isla pulled into the gravel lot of her small, modest farm-house in Yaxley, Ohio. It was a nine-hundred-square-foot ranch-style home seated on three-and-a-half acres of land. Tucked behind a row of trees on a little side road, it gave her the illusion of privacy and countryside without actually being too far away from civilization—or the police station, should she ever need it.

She had to admit it wasn't much, but it was home.

Sighing, Isla threw the gear in park and swung the door of her Honda CRV open. It was Sunday afternoon, which meant the coffee shop would've hit a lull. Although she'd missed the last few days, she didn't feel compelled to drag herself into work. Between the funeral, the failed IVF transfer, and the Secret Santa reemergence, she was mentally exhausted.

Not to mention, she was also still nursing a hangover, but that's what happened when she drank cheap liquor at age thirty.

Groaning, she dragged her suitcase across the rolling stones and bound her way up the stairs to unlock her front door.

Except, she didn't have a chance to unlock it because someone else had already done so.

"What the—"

Eyes wide, Isla gripped the handle on her luggage, her heart rate accelerating at an exponential speed. No one else had a key to her home, not even David, her ex-husband. She had the locks replaced after their divorce so he couldn't show up unannounced.

Regretting the choice to leave her pistol in the upstairs safe, Isla did a quick scan of her surroundings. She spotted her old fire poker lying underneath the windowsill and stealthily made her way toward it, careful not to make too much noise. With her eyes still peeled wide, she wrapped her fingers around the cold metal, ensured her phone was hidden in her pocket, and slowly pushed the door open.

At first glance, nothing looked out of place. The scattered pots and pans she didn't manage to wash before leaving were still sitting lopsided in the sink, the mail she'd dropped when she got the call about Rebecca was still sitting on the floor at the bottom of her stairs, and the light in her guest bathroom was still on.

Except—had she left the light on in the bathroom before she left? She was slightly messy, but she was diligent about turning off the lights to try and save on electricity. Her monthly bill was outrageous for this tiny house.

Inching forward, she took another calculated step toward the room. If she were watching a horror movie right now, this would be the part where the audience yelled, telling her not to do it—not to go in alone. To run outside the other way and call the cops while she waited safely in her car or at a neighbor's house.

But this wasn't a horror movie.

This was Isla's life, and despite the warnings she'd grown up with, something inside of her felt compelled to investigate. To know what was waiting for her inside that room, lurking inside the very depths of her home.

She was terrified, but she also felt a small adrenaline rush as she braved another step, raising her arm, fire poker at the ready.

She'd reached the end of the hallway now, her body just mere inches from the door, and that's when she saw it: a shadow behind the door.

Holy shit.

She watched as it moved just out of the cusp of view, and her body halted, warning her.

Fight or flight, Isla.

Which will it be?

With a deep, shaky breath, Isla waited until the count of three and then kicked in the door, blood pumping in her veins like an angry, violent storm.

"Holy shit, Isla! Can't a girl poop in privacy?"

Isla let out an exaggerated breath and dropped the stoker, wincing when it clattered against the cold, tiled ground. She bent over, hands on her knees and a bead of sweat sliding down her neck, as her best friend, Juniper, continued to ramble.

"You quite literally scared the shit out of me! Geez, Isla, what the hell are you doing sneaking up on people with that thing?"

"Me?" Isla retorted, looking up now with a bewildered look on her face. "What the hell are you doing taking a shit in my house?"

She stood up and brushed her pants before exiting the room and halting outside the door, knowing their conversation would continue through the partially open door.

"I needed a break from my roommate," Juniper said, her voice loud over the flush and then the sound of running water. "There's only so many times I can listen to her complain about her boyfriend yet do nothing about it."

Isla grasped her chest, her heart still beating wildly. "How'd you get inside?"

The door opened, and Juniper stepped out. Unlike the friends Isla had just left, June was like a breath of fresh air. A five-foot-three, strawberry-blonde representation of Isla's new life, where she was a successful business owner and a newly minted, strong, independent woman. Not the mean, sinful, snarky girl of her past.

"Please," June said. "I'm your best friend. You think I don't know where you keep the spare key hidden?" She raised a skeptical brow and walked past Isla to the living room, where an open bottle of 19 Crimes in Snoop Dog's Cali red blend sat on the coffee table. Isla hadn't noticed it before.

She checked the time on the microwave. "It's two o'clock."

Juniper, who had already curled herself back up on Isla's couch, rolled her head to the side, giving her best friend a knowing look. "Like I said, I needed to get away from my roommate." She paused to take a sip and then nodded to the bottle. "Want some?"

As if on cue, Isla's head throbbed, warning her again of what happens when you drink cheap booze at thirty, but given the current state of her life, she also didn't care.

Besides, wasn't there an old phrase that said this was the proper way to cure hangovers? Hair of the dog, or something like that?

Isla grabbed an empty glass from her cupboard and sank onto the couch opposite Juniper. "Gimme."

Juniper held out the bottle and then grabbed a bag of snacks from her purse. "Here," she said, shoving the candy in Isla's hand. "You look like you need these, too."

"Gee, thanks, June," Isla retorted.

Juniper shrugged. "Just being honest. That's the true mark of a best friend—someone who will tell you if your dress makes you look fat." She paused, popping another bite of chocolate-covered almonds in her mouth. "Politely, you know. Best of intentions."

Isla rolled her eyes and took a bite, followed by a sip of the dry wine.

"So," Juniper started, "how was it?"

Isla sighed and rubbed her forehead. "How do you think?"

June's face twisted, much like the messy French braid falling from her claw clip. "That bad, huh?"

Nodding, Isla grabbed another handful of snacks and sat the bag down, already regretting her decision not to pick up Chinese on the way home. If she was going to break her diet for chocolate and wine, she might as well have gotten the takeout she wanted instead of promising to eat the rotting vegetables in her fridge.

"It was awful . . ." Isla's words trailed as she thought back to Becca's corpse. "Her body was so frail, her face so bruised. She looked fake and . . . malevolent. Like an unnatural wax model that someone threw away from an abandoned department store."

"Damn, girl," Juniper breathed. "I'm so sorry you had to go through that."

Isla swirled another drink in her mouth, letting the liquid prickle on her tongue. "Thanks." She sat in silence for another moment before adding, "The others were there, too."

Juniper leaned back against her pillow, a questioning look on her face. "Oh?"

"Yeah," Isla continued. "Everyone from our friend group."

"Oh, shit," Juniper said, this time more understanding. "Even the travel influencer?"

Isla nodded. "Yep. Even Carley."

A loud noise sounded from the staircase, and moments later, a black cat named Moon padded into view. Isla tried not to pay mind to the twenty-minute delayed welcome, along with the lack of concern after the bathroom scenario—guard cat he was not—but then again, no cat really cared about their human more than themselves. It's what separated them from dogs.

And some humans.

She scratched his head, contemplating her words. "They want to get back together for Secret Santa again."

Juniper gasped, her blue eyes wide and vibrant. "Shut up."

"Yup. I tried to say no, but"—she paused, popping another piece of candy in her mouth—"I was so drunk. No one listened to me. Before I knew it, I was staring at Scarlett's name on a scrap piece of paper."

"No way, really?" Her friend's jaw was nearly on the floor as she untangled her limbs, stretching and stealing the cat from Isla's lap. The traitor didn't even flinch. "I can't believe that."

Neither could Isla. Sure, a small part of her was excited about the revival of her favorite pastime, but that same part was also shrouded by trauma.

Grief.

Another beat passed while Isla processed the vastness of it all, appreciating the space Juniper held for her. It was what she loved most about their friendship—the ability to comfortably sit in the silence, the sadness, the madness—hell, the internal and external chaos of it all.

The world needed more friends like Juniper.

"I should just cancel."

June furrowed her brow as she took another sip from her glass. "I thought you loved this tradition, though."

"I did," Isla concurred. No sense in denying it.

But then came the real question, the one Isla dreaded answering.

"So then, why cancel? It sounds like fun."

There were so many reasons Isla could share.

The one she decided to divulge was this:

"The IVF didn't work."

That was the truth Juniper could accept the most.

"Oh, Isla," her friend said, lowering her glass and handful of candy. "Girl, I am so sorry. Oh my gosh, I didn't even think when I offered you the wine."

Isla bit the inside of her lip, willing the tears to stay hidden behind faux eyelash extensions. "It's fine." She sniffed and adjusted in her seat, not wanting to show her emotions for fear of being too vulnerable. Too annoying. Too much of herself in a way that she could never take back.

"I, um," she said, clearing her throat again. "It was a stupid idea anyway. I should've known better. It's what I get for trying to use our last embryo without talking to David first."

When Isla finally raised her eyes to meet Juniper's gaze, she saw a misty version of herself reflected in June's blue irises. "Honey—"

Isla stopped her. "Seriously, it's fine. The baby would've been a Leo, and I don't know much about the signs, but I think that means she would've been a total attention seeker." Isla laughed, trying to deflect from her pain, but Juniper didn't miss a beat, her voice soft when she spoke.

"You think she would've been a girl." It was a statement, not a question.

Isla stared at her friend as the revelation of the words hit her. "Yeah," she said with a weak voice. "A girl. And she would've ruled the fucking world."

She let her emotional walls down as the tears broke through her metaphorical dam.

SCARLETT
Now

LIGHTS. ALCOHOL. LOADED QUESTIONS and insincere compliments.

It was always the same at her husband's charity events. Scarlett had grown to hate them.

She was currently waiting for dinner to be served while Governor Tim Pumice went on and on about his damn dog. Scarlett could understand if the event was for animals, but since it wasn't, the man had no business bringing that bulldog on stage. Especially since Calvin's office had politely asked him not to. If this man could just follow the fucking guidelines . . .

An abrupt applause broke out, startling Scarlett from her thoughts. She sipped her wine, careful not to mess up her lipstick.

"Isn't his dog such a charmer?" the woman to her right asked. "It's so nice seeing a respectable, down-to-earth man in office."

Scar had to fight the urge to roll her eyes. "Yes, it is something."

She watched as the woman opened her mouth to respond, but Calvin intervened, cutting her off. For once, Scarlett was grateful for her husband.

"What did you think of the lamb, Mrs. Benson?"

The woman's eyes lit up, and Scarlett tuned them out as they discussed the Swedish appetizer Scar had single-handedly picked, along with the entire menu, for this event. They were trying to raise money for a new children's hospital, and Scarlett knew they needed something elegant yet rooted in the state's heritage if they wanted to tug on donors' heartstrings. That's why she'd contacted the owner of The Hütte Restaurant from Helvetia, the state's destination Swedish village, asking if they'd cater. It was located in the heart of Appalachia and had just enough *je ne sais quoi* to impress the night's guests.

Not that her husband had thanked her or anything as he lapped up her successful idea, shmoozing the smitten old woman. It made her want to gag.

She reached for her glass of wine again, and a wave of pain shot through her abdomen. Grimacing, Scarlett retracted her hand and excused herself to the restroom. It had been a week since the D and C procedure, and although the doctor said her bleeding and cramping should have stopped by now, she was still experiencing major bouts of pain.

Cursing, she slammed the door open to the ladies' room, nearly dumping her entire purse out on the counter in search of pain relievers. She knew she shouldn't have come tonight. It was too soon. That's what she'd told Calvin when she'd asked him, begged him if she could stay home, but he'd insisted she be there.

"I can't attend my own fundraiser without my wife on my arm," he'd said as he stood in the doorway. "How do you think that would look? I mean,"—he tilted his head, scoffing—"can you imagine what the tabloids would say?"

Scarlett had desperately tried to hold back her tears as she clung to her empty womb. "Please, Calvin. I'm still in so much pain."

"You'll be fine." He'd walked to the mirror then, straightening his tie. "You just have to mentally lock it away. Then you'll feel better."

"I don't mean *mentally.*" She'd sneered the word, detesting how weak he made her sound. "I'm physically in pain from having our dead child scraped from my loins a few days ago! Can't you see that?" Her breath had gone ragged at that point, her voice breaking at the question.

Calvin had looked over his shoulder then, pausing as he likely considered her words. For a moment, Scarlett felt a small seed of hope blooming in her chest.

But then he squashed it, stomping on her heart in the process. "We just need to get through tonight. Then you can take it easy over the weekend. I promise."

Scarlett splashed water on her face now, trying to distract herself from the ache in her chest and the spasms in her stomach. How did she get here? Bending to the will of a man and crying unshed tears over a child she would never know? She was Scarlett Miller, for crying out loud. She was supposed to conquer the world, become the first female president, change lives. She never wanted *this*. It was all just supposed to be a detour, a means to position herself better in the political world so that when the time came, she'd have a higher success rate of winning the gubernatorial race. The concept of playing the dutiful wife had always disgusted her, but she'd be damned if she wasn't going to play the system, the same way it tried to play her.

She just never expected to get pregnant from her little rendezvous with their financial advisor, Julio, much less lose the child and actually *feel* something for it. When that pregnancy test showed up positive, she thought her biggest issue would be explaining the affair to Calvin once he realized the baby's skin color didn't match his own. She hadn't imagined a reality worse than that, yet here it was.

Just then, her phone pinged from where she'd dumped it on the sink. She groaned, not in the mood to talk to anyone but checking it nonetheless.

The Snitches

Wren: *Where did y'all wanna eat for our Secret Santa dinner?? We never decided!*

Liam: *Please don't say Thick Chicks . . .*

Wren: *LOL definitely not*

Scarlett rolled her eyes. Of course they weren't going to Thick Chicks. Batting away another tear, she thumbed out a quick response.

Scarlett: *Of course not. Don't be ridiculous. We'll go to Bella Cucina's like always. It was Rebecca's favorite.*

Carley: *Was it? I always thought she chose that place to impress us. If we really are doing this to honor her memory, maybe we should choose somewhere that was more *her* vibe, ya know?*

Scarlett shifted her weight, annoyed Carley was challenging her.

Scarlett: *What, you think we should go to Sheetz, get a pepperoni roll maybe?*

It was a dig, but she didn't care.

Isla: *Actually, pizza was her favorite food.*

Wren: *Oooh! That's right. What about Evan's?*

Evan's Pizza? Absolutely not. There was no way Scarlett was eating there. The thought instantly sobered her, distracting from her pain.

Carley: *I love that idea!*

Scarlett: *No way. Haven't you seen their health inspection circulating all over the internet? We are not going there.*

She shook her head as her friends continued to fire off texts, one after another, arguing about whether that was legit.

Suddenly, a new idea popped into Scarlett's mind, and she felt a hint of excitement as she typed out the message.

Scarlett: *Why don't you guys come to my place? I can host and have my chef cook for us.*

She stared at her phone, a smile forming on her lips at the idea. It had been ages since she'd hosted something just for the fun of it, without family or politicians or obligations. This would give her a chance to unwind and possibly reconnect with the others in the group. She'd been on an island for so long, but seeing her husband's response to her in the wake of a miscarriage made Scarlett realize that maybe it was time to have someone else in her corner. Someone she didn't have to keep hidden like a dirty secret.

Liam: *As long as it's not Chef Boyardee Pizza . . .*

Scarlett actually snorted.

Scarlett: *Good then. It's settled. My place, Saturday, December 21st at 6 p.m. We'll have drinks and apps, then dinner, followed by the gift exchange.*

She clicked her phone shut, satisfied with her decision.

This would be fun, therapeutic even.

The perfect distraction, one that didn't involve sex with her financial advisor.

LIAM
NOW

"I STILL DON'T UNDERSTAND why you're doing this."

Liam let out an exasperated sigh as his husband, Ben, popped out the cork on a new bottle of chardonnay as they relaxed in their New York condo.

"I told you," Liam started, "we're doing it in honor of Rebecca's memory."

Ben quirked a brow and pinched his lips. "I don't believe that. This has drama written all over it, and you know it."

Hearing a noise, Liam peeked at the baby monitor. After ensuring both of the twins were still asleep, he turned back to Ben, already exhausted from this conversation. He loved his husband, but Ben always thought he knew best. Arguing with him was like going to war, and Liam didn't feel like picking a battle today. He wanted to relax under a nice warm blanket and drift off lazily to sleep.

"It's been almost ten years." He paused, taking a sip of the white wine, savoring the light taste on his tongue. "And honestly, I have no beef with anyone. We were just kids back then. I'd like to think everyone has matured and we can be civil."

What could he say? Their roots ran deep. Liam had grown up with these women. Everyone but Isla had gone to the same elementary school, and after discovering who they were in those awful middle school years, their friendships clicked into place. They were the first ones to accept him when he came out, showing fierce loyalty any time one of their redneck classmates attempted to make fun of him.

"We've worked out our shit," he added, letting out another deep breath. "And they were always there for me when I needed them, especially Isla and Bec."

Ben shook his head, still unconvinced. "Well, I don't trust Scarlett, *at all*, or even Wren for that matter. A woman who can birth that many kids and not lose her mind is unnatural." He retrieved the bag of popcorn from the microwave before the beeping could start, careful not to disturb the babies. "I guess Carley's alright. Why can't you just do this with her and Isla? Or do something else?"

Liam contemplated his husband's words for a moment. It wasn't a terrible idea, actually, but he'd feel rude excluding Scarlett and Wren. "We were all friends with Rebecca. She wouldn't want us to be catty toward one another."

As the words came off his tongue, he knew they were true. Rebecca had always been their glue—the one who held them together and made them look past their differences for the greater good of the group. They'd lost touch with so many others after high school, and Becca was determined to keep the six of them together, claiming they'd always been *it*, whatever that meant.

"Can we just watch the movie?" Liam asked, pivoting. "I'm tired and just wanna relax."

Before Ben could answer, though, Liam's phone went off.

"Speak of the devil," Ben said, brows raised as he peeked at the phone and then slid it toward Liam, who quickly groaned.

The Snitches

Scarlett: Check your emails, snitches! Everyone should have been sent the shared Google doc where you can input your Christmas wish list for this season.

Conflicting feelings roared in Liam's chest. He'd just said he was exhausted, and he meant it, but this had always been his favorite part of their tradition. He loved shopping for his Secret Santa, and curating his own wish list, if he was being honest.

Thumbing out a quick response, he closed out the app and grabbed his laptop from the kitchen island.

"What is it?" Ben asked as Liam drummed his fingers against the granite countertop.

"Scarlett sent the Google doc for us to add our wish list." Liam tapped the link as a familiar rush of nostalgia came flooding back. "We used to write these by hand back in high school—on a shared piece of notebook paper everyone passed around."

"Wait," Ben said, popping a kernel in his mouth. "So you guys tell each other what to buy?"

Liam considered his question. "Not specifically. We just share our favorite things, like scents, stores, candies, interests. Anything really. That way, your Santa has something to go off of in case you draw someone you're not as close with." He paused, thinking about how they were all basically strangers this year. "It just helps keep things simple."

A rush of warm air flooded the small apartment as the heater kicked on.

"What's the budget?" Ben asked, saddling up on the stool next to Liam.

Again, Liam paused. "I don't . . . know exactly."

His husband looked at him, a skeptical look on his face. "What do you mean you don't know? That's, like, the first rule of Secret Santa. Everyone knows that. You can't have one of you spending twenty-five bucks while someone else blows one hundred dollars or pulls a Michael Scott, buying an iPod."

Liam shook his head at Ben's theatrics. "I mean, we used to have one for that reason. It started out small when we were freshmen, of course. The twenty-to-fifty range, I think. We stayed in that ballpark for a while, but then, as the years went on, we slowly raised it." His lips twitched at the distant memory as it nudged at the forefront of his brain. "Then a couple of us got retail jobs and started getting these incredible discounts on high-end stuff. We kind of stopped keeping track of dollar amounts at that point. Everyone just shopped for their person the best they could, knowing fully well that each Secret Santa would shower the other with love and luxuries. It was like Christmas morning—but on crack."

An odd sensation tugged at his heart as he thought about the last gift exchange they'd done during their sophomore year at RHU, completely unaware it would be their last one. Everyone had been in such a good mood at the restaurant, and Becca had spoiled the group afterward at Scar's place. He remembered staying up until three or four in the morning with her after the others passed out, drunkenly giggling and eating cookies as they watched *Clueless*. It was one of his favorite memories.

"Jiminy Cricket," Ben said, pulling Liam from his trance. "Y'all spent a lot of money for a group of friends who talked shit about each other behind each other's backs."

"Yeah," Liam said, his voice distant. "But it was magical."

And detrimental.

But he didn't say that out loud.

Ben sighed again, pulling the wine bottle toward them. "All right," he said, wrapping an arm around Liam's bicep. "Change of plans."

Liam slid his eyes to meet Ben's gaze, a question on his face.

"We can't possibly watch a movie now." Ben nodded to the screen. "Come on. Pull up Pinterest, Macy's, the local shops, all the places. Let's make a Christmas wish list."

ISLA
NOW

"Order for Lindsey."

Isla placed two iced sugar cookie lattes, an eggnog chai, and a peppermint scone on the counter. Business had been picking up even more so than usual, likely on account of the holiday season. Everyone wanted their sugar and caffeine fix before shopping, and with tomorrow being Thanksgiving, Isla didn't blame them.

She smiled at the tall brunette who picked up the order, and then her heart skipped a beat when she saw the blonde little girl next to her decked out in a velvet red dress and black tights, all coordinating with the matching bow atop her head. She was beautiful, maybe three years old, and had her eyes glued on the scone as her mom retrieved the goodies from the counter.

Isla felt sick.

The Monday after she got home from Rebecca's funeral, she saw her fertility doctor, where she was met with the overwhelming confirmation that she would never be pregnant. Not unless she did another egg retrieval and used a donor sperm, but even then, her chances were low. She had endometriosis and PCOS, not one but two conditions that made it nearly impossible for her to conceive.

It's what you deserve, her inner voice whispered.

"Be right back." She shoved her headset off and nearly ran to the stockroom, her pulse racing as the insides of her chest threatened to crack.

Breathe.

Just breathe.

The devastation of it all came flooding back, and even though she hadn't technically grown a child in her womb, she felt an emptiness in the pit of her stomach that told a different story.

Crying, she hugged her hand to her belly and then started flicking the hair bow on her wrist, attempting to ground herself back to reality.

"Boss?"

A voice sounded from the other side of the door, and Isla wiped her hands across her face.

"Yeah?"

"The Girl Scout troop is here for their ornament exchange." It was Sam, her barista. "They're asking for you."

Nodding, Isla took a controlled, deep breath. "Okay. I'll be right there."

She'd completely forgotten about agreeing to let the local troop use the back area for their Christmas ornament exchange party; she could think of nothing worse to deal with at this exact moment.

Sighing, she patted her face with a little flour, attempting to hide the redness in her cheeks, and emerged from the storage closet. Then, she marched out to the lobby and prepared for an afternoon of staring at cute children.

HOURS LATER, WHEN THE last of the Girl Scouts had finished their chocolate frappes and cake pops, Isla breathed a sigh of relief as she cleaned up the last of their mess. It hadn't been as bad as she thought it would be having them in the shop all afternoon. Once she got over the initial grief, she actually found herself enjoying their company. Their little giggles and screams added a warm sense of merriment to the cafe. By the end of it, Isla was both content and exhausted. She was ready to sink into her sofa and fall asleep to the soothing sound of trash TV, but seeing as she had a three-hour drive back to West Virginia in the morning, that wasn't an option. She still had to pack, clean her house, and figure out something to bring for her mom's Thanksgiving dinner.

Not to mention the dozen or so tasks she still had to do for the shop.

As an entrepreneur, Isla never had much downtime. Being the owner meant she was also the head baker, trainer, lead barista, shop manager, marketing guru, HR manager, and any other title you could think of, albeit accountant. Isla was infinitely bad at numbers. They just didn't come naturally to her, and it was the only thing she felt confident outsourcing.

Her brain fried, she tried running back through her mental checklist. Everything at the store had already been prepped for her staff's Black Friday return, but she had a handful of marketing and admin tasks to complete. There were social media posts and email campaigns to schedule, along with several donation requests to respond to before she left.

After popping her neck and arching her back, Isla turned toward her office to retrieve her laptop when she heard a noise. It sounded like . . . tapping. Like someone was tapping on the front door, or maybe the window. She swiveled back around on her heel and headed to the front of the lobby, prepared to shoo off an irate customer, but when she reached the glass door, no one was there.

Huh.

She supposed it could've just been a tree branch stretching on something or maybe the pizza shop next door, but a prickling sensation on the back of her neck told her otherwise. Isla's gut twisted as she spun again and made her way through the entire shop, checking every room and glancing out each window, but in the end, she came up short, no closer to finding the source of the noise.

"Probably just the pizza guys cleaning something," she said out loud, reassuring herself.

So then why do you still feel like someone is watching you?

Nervous, she considered grabbing her car keys and leaving, but just then, her phone pinged from its spot on the coffee counter. She took a few calming breaths, reminding herself she was just being paranoid, then grabbed her phone and flipped it over.

Shock and excitement registered over her face when she saw Carley and Liam's names in a new group chat.

Carley: *Hey guys!! Wanted to get your opinion on something.*

Isla twisted her lips to the side, curiosity getting the best of her as her previous fears continued to dissipate. With Carley, an opening statement like that could really mean anything.

Isla: *What's up?*

Liam: *Go on . . .*

A slow minute passed as Isla waited for her response, and she noted the noise from earlier had stopped.

Carley: *Well, I know we're doing Secret Santa again and all, but I kinda wanna do something else for Bec. What do you guys think about a weekend trip to Greenbrier this spring?*

Isla smiled as she stared at the screen. Rebecca's family didn't have a lot of money growing up, so her grandparents would try to whisk her away by taking her camping. It was usually to local places, like Beech Cliffs or Grover Caves, but she'd always raved about one magical summer when her grandpa took them to Greenbrier. Not the fancy hotel but the county itself. Bec told them stories of going tubing in the river, picking fresh raspberries for pancakes every morning, and fishing with her GrandPop until they'd burned up all the daylight. Isla had never desired to go there, but she smiled at her friend's memories nonetheless.

Isla: *I think that's perfect. Bec would've loved it.*

Liam: *100%*

Liam: *Do it*

Carley: *Eeeeeek! I knew you guys would love it. Consider this your open invitation to join me!!*

Isla cocked her head as she stared at the screen. She personally hated the idea of camping, but maybe she could rent a cabin.

Liam: *We could probs borrow my mom's camper actually.*

A camper. Isla considered the idea for a moment.

Isla: *I guess I wouldn't be opposed to glamping.*

Carley's response was immediate.

Carley: *Perf! Let's plan it. Maybe we can meet up to chat before the Secret Santa dinner? I don't really wanna invite the other two. Not to be mean, but like, you know how they are.*

Isla snorted.

Liam: *Planning sesh/pregame drinks at Thick Chicks then?*

Isla: *Sounds good to me!*

Carley: *Eeeeeek! This is gonna be dope, y'all. My followers will love it.*

A sudden irritation lapped at Isla's skin. Of course Carley wanted to feature the trip on her social pages. She was a travel influencer—it's what she did. So what if it cheapened the memory of their dead best friend?

Isla: *Gotta finish up some work. Hope you guys have a good Thanksgiving.*

She locked her phone, not bothering to read their responses. She really did have work to do.

Turning back to her office, she grabbed the laptop off her desk and returned to the lobby, folding herself into the cozy leather chair by the Christmas tree.

Nearly an hour later, she yawned and stretched her legs, satisfied with the day's work and thoughts of her friends long forgotten. She was about to tidy up her small mess and leave when something peculiar caught her eye.

There, hanging just below a unicorn ornament one of the girls had left, was a folded piece of paper tucked into a branch.

Hmm.

"That's weird." Curious, Isla sat her laptop down on the floor and stood. She reached for the parchment, wondering if one of the girls left it there by accident.

Smiling as she prepared herself for a thank you note or perhaps a doodle, she unfolded the paper.

And then her heart stopped working.

Unto us a child is born

In an instant, Isla felt her entire world shift beneath her. A paradigm effect to the reality she'd been so desperately trying to escape.

Eyes wide and searching, she scanned the lobby again as her heart raced.

Bright flashes of red blurred her vision, the memory of the blood all but consuming her.

"No," she breathed, crinkling the paper in her hand.

There's no way anyone could know about that night.

It was impossible.

And yet . . .

She uncrumbled the tattered note, scanning it again for signs of something, anything that would indicate this was a joke.

But all she saw were the six little words staring back at her, written in red and dripping like crimson blood from Santa's sleigh.

REBECCA
THEN

"HEY, ISLA?" REBECCA WRUNG her hands in front of her as she stood in the doorway to Isla's room. "Can we talk?"

Isla looked up from her desk where she'd been studying for finals. "What's up?"

What's up? Such a simple question for such a complicated answer. Maybe she should tell Scarlett instead. She'd been there that night after all. She would believe her.

No. Tell her.

"Umm . . ." Rebecca hesitated, clearing her throat. She needed to do this. She'd been trying to tell Isla about what happened with David for the last two months, but every time she tried, she froze.

Like she was doing now.

The words getting tangled in her mouth, she heaved her shoulders back and decided to show Isla what she'd been hiding in her back pocket. Without another word, she sat on the bed in the middle of the room and slid the test across the covers, revealing two pink lines.

For a moment, Isla stared at it, eyes wide. Then, finally, she said, "You're . . . pregnant?"

Rebecca nodded.

The look on Isla's face was a mix of shock and confusion. "H-how? Who?"

There it was—Becca's opportunity, served on a silver platter. She should just rip off the Band-Aid. Tell her now while she still had the courage.

Instead, she said, "I don't know. Just some guy."

Shame flooded her as she internally scolded herself. The words had been there, right on the tip of her tongue, but for whatever reason, she couldn't bring herself to tell Isla that her boyfriend had drugged and raped her, resulting in pregnancy.

Rebecca didn't know why she felt this way. David was the one who should be ashamed, not her.

She hated feeling guilty for reasons she couldn't quite comprehend.

"Holy shit, Bec." Isla moved to sit on the bed too. "Are you okay?"

Tears formed at Rebecca's lash line, and she shook her head. "No, not really." She wanted to say so much more but couldn't.

Isla continued to stare at her, bewildered. "Did you guys not use protection?"

The words stung Becca to her core. As if she had a choice in the matter.

Instead of responding, she shrugged her shoulders.

Scratching above her eyebrow, Isla asked, "What are you going to do?"

Becca laid back on Isla's bed and noted the steady whirl of the ceiling fan. Her eyes traced it as it went round and round, much like her mind.

"I don't know," she said after a minute.

The fan continued to twirl, the only sound in the room as silence filled the space.

Its presence was suffocating.

You can still tell her, Becca's inner voice whispered. *She will understand. She's your best friend.*

"Do you," Isla started, her voice interrupting the quiet, "want to keep it?"

Shock rang through Rebecca's core, and she sat up straight. Of course she did. She may not be a perfect Christian by any means, but she didn't believe in abortion.

"I'm not going to kill my baby, Isla."

Isla's gaze softened. "I know you wouldn't. I was talking about adoption."

"Oh," Rebecca said, the previous edge in her tone now softened. "I don't know."

She tried to think of something else to say, but words escaped her. There was so much to process. So much to comprehend.

"Have you told anyone else?" Isla asked.

Becca answered quickly, panic rising at the thought. "No. And I don't think I'm going to." The words continued to roll off her tongue without thought. "Can you imagine what the others would say? What my mother would say?"

What David would say.

Her eyes widened at the thought, and suddenly, Rebecca regretted having told Isla at all.

"Isla," she said, her voice urgent. "Promise me you won't say anything. Anything at all. Especially to the others or . . ." She hesitated, the taste of his name on her tongue nauseating. "David. Please don't tell David." And then for good measure, she added, "No one can know."

Worry lines began to crease on Isla's forehead, but Rebecca already knew she would keep her secret.

Isla was a good friend.

Her best friend.

"Okay," Isla said after a beat of silence, proving her loyalty. "I promise. I won't say anything."

SCARLETT
NOW

SCARLETT CHOPPED THE SWEET potatoes with a vengeance as Wren bustled around her, talking a mile a minute about her children.

"I mean, don't get me wrong. I love staying home with them. It's such a blessing, but I also just feel like I'm going to lose my damn mind a little bit if Brennan doesn't stop working such late hours."

Phantom kicks fluttered in Scarlett's womb, and she sliced another sweet potato. "Just get a nanny."

Wren looked at her as if she'd been slapped. "I can't do that. I'm a stay-at-home mom." She opened the fridge, retrieving a carton of orange juice. "I'm the nanny. That's my job. Along with the maid, chef, chauffeur."

Scarlett resisted the urge to roll her eyes as Wren rambled on. "You could go back to work if you're so miserable being with your children."

Wren's eyes widened, and she coughed, nearly choking on her drink. "I'm not *miserable*. I'm just venting. Geez, what's gotten into you lately?"

"Nothing," Scarlett replied, dumping the potatoes in a pot of boiling water. She shouldn't be so snippy with Wren. It's not like she knew about Scarlett's miscarriage, but standing here, listening to her complain about her four healthy, living children and a husband who actually cares about her—and doesn't cheat—made her temper flare.

Pressing her fingers to her temple, she sighed, wondering how long it would be until she could see Julio again. She had never meant to sleep with him, honestly. As their financial advisor, he had simply been a nice human to look at. Someone drastically different than her husband, but handsome nonetheless. He wasn't the tallest, but his stocky build and tan skin made up for it, as did his bald head and tattoos. The moment Scar discovered Calvin was sleeping with his secretary, she stalked into Julio's office and made him an offer he couldn't refuse.

Scarlett ran her tongue across the back of her teeth to keep from smiling at the thought. It all really was unlike her. She'd even begged Calvin to fire Julio at first.

"He looks like a drug dealer," she'd said one evening during dinner. "You can't honestly trust him with our finances. He's probably using us to wash his own dirty money."

Calvin had scolded her, though, saying he was an old friend, one he'd trust with his life.

Too bad he couldn't trust the man with his wife.

She took a deep breath and set the timer for twenty minutes before stealing the orange juice carton from Wren and dumping it into a glass and topping it off with champagne. Wren raised a brow at Scar as her eyes flicked to the clock, but Scarlett defended herself before she could say anything.

"It's Thanksgiving morning. I'm just stressed." Scar shrugged as she threw the champagne flute back, hoping her words were convincing. "Plus," she added after gulping down her drink, "Calvin's monster-in-law is coming this year."

"Ah," Wren said, bobbing her head as she tried to hide a smile. "That's why you're playing Sally Homemaker instead of having your chef prepare this."

"Don't be silly," Scarlett snapped. "I'm only doing the sweet potato casserole. I don't trust those imbeciles with Mama's recipe. They never get it right, and I don't feel like listening to Betty complain."

Wren snorted. "I don't blame you, I guess. Mine drove me nuts last night while I was prepping everything." She paused before adding, "Another reason I had to get out of the house."

At that comment, Scar reached for the bottle of champagne again, this time not bothering with the orange juice. She supposed that was one perk of no longer being pregnant: self-medicating was back on the table.

Pivoting, she turned back to Wren. "Have you started shopping for your Secret Santa yet?"

Wren's face lit up. "Nope. I've been waiting for this weekend. My person has . . . lavish tastes, and I wanna make sure I get them something good."

Now it was Scarlett's turn to snort. "So you have me?"

"No," Wren said, surprising her. "I have someone else this year." She stood from her place at the kitchen island and stretched. "You know, I was sad at first that we didn't have a chance to rig it like we used to, but it's been kinda fun focusing on a different person in the group for a change."

Scarlett chose to omit the fact that she tried to do their old trick by selecting the largest piece of paper in the bag but was disappointed when Wren's name wasn't on it. "I thought you forgot about that."

"I mean, I guess I did until after it was too late. That night was such a whirlwind."

Scarlett nodded, memories of that night resurfacing. She still couldn't believe she'd agreed to go along with this crazy idea to reinstate the tradition. It'd been fun, sure, but nothing she swooned over as much as her friends did. Although, now that she thought about it, a small part of her was proud of doing it. Rebecca deserved to be remembered beyond some bogus funeral and a phony night of drinks where everyone pretended they hadn't fallen out of touch for the last decade. Secret Santa had always been the highlight of their year, and when Rebecca didn't reach out to anyone to discuss the plan during their junior year, she knew things would never be the same between their misfit group.

Scarlett blamed the jerk who took advantage of Becca that awful night at the Kappa Sigma house. She could still remember the moment she walked in that bedroom like it was yesterday. The beaten, battered version of Becca lying naked and scared on the cold floor, streaks of blood running down her legs. Scarlett knew in an instant what had happened.

She hated that Rebecca never told her who it was.

Tracing a condensation line as it slipped down the side of her glass, she remained lost in her thoughts until Wren cleared her throat.

"I'd better go." She threw her oversized purse over her shoulder. "The turkey needs to be basted, and I don't trust my husband."

Scarlett started to make a rude comment, but a crash sounded from the dining room, interrupting her line of thought.

"What the hell?" Scar sat down her glass and beelined through the kitchen into the next room.

"What was that?" Wren called, following close behind.

When Scarlett entered the doorway, her jaw nearly dropped. "Someone smashed my window."

The sight stunned her.

Wren continued to ramble, but Scarlett tuned her out, moving toward the shattered opening. At first, she didn't see anything other than the pile of glass, but upon closer inspection, she realized the shards were burying something underneath.

And they were coated in flecks of red.

72

"Calvin!" she yelled, a combination of anger and fear licking at her chest. Who the hell had the audacity to throw something through her vintage, single-pane window? And on a *holiday*. As a politician's wife, she'd endured her fair share of theatrics—people throwing napkins and paper wads at them in public, the occasional yelling match at the grocery store, and even light stalking from one woman who was obsessed with her husband. But no one had ever gone so far as to cause damage to their property. Clearly, she needed to upgrade their security measures.

When her husband didn't respond—no surprise there—she looked around, wondering what the main character in one of the thriller novels that she liked to read would do.

"Oh my gosh!" Wren squeaked from behind. "Oh my gosh, oh my gosh. We need to call the police."

And tell them what? Scarlett thought.

She glanced at the pile again, then decided a smart protagonist would investigate the accident further before jumping to conclusions. Spotting a cloth napkin on the table, she snatched it off the place setting and wrapped her hand in it.

"What are you doing?" Wren sounded like a basket case.

Scarlett responded dryly. "We need to see what it is."

Without any further explanation, she dug through the shards of glass, careful not to move too quickly. It took a moment to reach the item, but when she did, she wrapped her fingers around it, extracting it gently. It was too light to be a brick. Honestly, it was too light to smash her window at all unless this person was right beside the house.

Shaking off the last glass fragments from the cloth, she unwrapped the fabric and was shocked to see a ceramic ornament of baby Jesus.

Lying in a manger.

Covered in blood.

REBECCA
THEN

A SINGLE SNOWFLAKE MELTED on Becca's lashes, and she blinked, wishing she could appreciate the beauty of the snow.

But instead, she was stranded on the side of the road with a busted tire.

So much for a holly, jolly Christmas.

She scoffed and blew a breath, wondering how she would get herself out of this predicament. It was Christmas Eve, and she was forty weeks pregnant with a secret baby. The only people who knew about the child were Isla and her midwife. There was no way she was telling her junkie of a mother that she got knocked up, even if the pregnancy was a result of rape and not her own misdoings. Her mother would scold her, potentially slap her, and then chastise her for giving the baby up, even if it was the best thing for her and the child.

Rebecca was still on her mother's insurance, though, so she'd taken out additional student loans at the beginning of the semester to pay for a midwife out of pocket. This way, she could have a private, at-home birth, and her mom would never see a medical bill or insurance request. She may be in debt to the university forever, but keeping this whole thing private was worth it. She would simply call the Safe Haven number after the midwife left, give them her baby, and wash her hands of the whole thing.

Or so she thought.

A car rushed by, the *whoosh* reminding her of the current situation. She had no idea how to change a tire, nor did Isla. She doubted Clara, her midwife, knew either. Cursing under her breath, Becca hid back in the safety of her beaten-down car and pulled out her phone, calling Isla first, then Clara to ask for a ride. When neither answered, she grunted, toggling to her Safari search bar.

How to change a tire

The search results were unyielding, leaving her feeling more defeated than when she'd started. Clicking the phone shut, she tried to run through her options.

She could call a cab, but that would risk being kidnapped or murdered.

She could call her uncle, but that would risk him telling her mom about her *situation.*

Or she could get out and walk. She was only a few miles from her apartment, and the streets were deserted with it being Christmas Eve. Even if someone saw her, her coat was large enough to cover her bump, just making her look fat.

For a moment, she considered an alternate option where she stayed in her car for all eternity until she died, but assuming that was *irresponsible,* she took a deep breath and shoved her knit hat and gloves on.

"I guess we're taking a walk, Baby."

TWENTY MINUTES LATER, BECCA was—potentially—halfway closer to home. She would still have to figure out how to get her car back, but that was a problem for future Becca.

Taking a deep breath, she continued trudging her feet through the fallen snow, admiring the picturesque scene. Most of her friends hated living in Wilderby, but she loved it. Rebecca thought the city was perfectly situated between the mountainous hills of West Virginia, offering solace in a world of chaos. The light dusting of snow had already blanketed the city, giving it a soft, ethereal glow. Becca smiled as she wondered what the area would look like in the morning when everyone woke up and looked out their windows before retreating to open their presents from Santa and their loved ones.

And then she frowned, because she wouldn't get to do that this year. Didn't even get to celebrate her beloved Secret Santa tradition with her closest friends.

You chose to isolate yourself. It didn't have to be this way.

She brushed away a loose tear, silently chiding her thoughts. Of course it had to be this way. She couldn't even work up the nerve to tell Isla that David was the one who impregnated her. How was she supposed to face the questions of others if she couldn't even face her best friend?

Oof.

She stopped dead in her tracks for a moment, a tightening sensation overcoming her belly.

That was weird.

Rubbing a hand underneath her stomach, she felt the baby kick in response. Relieved, Becca popped her neck from side to side, then decided to keep moving.

"Ahh!"

Her gasp was audible this time as another wave of sensations struck her stomach.

"What the—"

And then in an instant, her entire world collapsed around her as a gush of warm water ran down her legs.

ISLA

NOW

Isla woke up on edge Thanksgiving morning for reasons she wasn't willing to address.

She'd simply found a song lyric that someone scribbled on a piece of paper—that's all it was, she decided.

No one was watching her, leaving her ominous notes on her store's Christmas tree. That would be absurd.

Today was a holiday, and she refused to let the ghosts of her past haunt her. She'd woken up at the crack of dawn to ensure she was on the road to arrive at her mom's early enough to help with the day-of preparations. Her mom was the type of woman who liked to work ahead and make the actual day as low-stress as possible, but Isla knew there were always little things here and there that needed to be done, and she was more than happy to help. It was the least she could do after everything her mom had done for her over the years.

Now, at a quarter until ten, she pulled into her childhood driveway in Wilderby and shifted the gear into park. Taking a moment to check her reflection in the mirror, she sighed and opened the car door, retrieving the pumpkin scones left over from the shop. They may not be super fresh, but it was the thought that counted.

Smoothing out her black sweater dress, she slammed the car door shut and bound up the stairs, not bothering to knock before entering.

"Hello?" she called, entering the foyer. "Mom? I'm home!"

A chorus of laughter erupted from the kitchen, and Isla scrunched her forehead. Her mom didn't usually have people over this early. Her Aunt Jess usually came in the afternoon when it was closer to dinner time, and that was about the extent of their immediate family.

Isla rounded the corner to the kitchen, and when she saw who was leaning against the counter, she froze.

"Hey, Cronkite. Long time no see."

Isla's heart fluttered at the sound of her old nickname on his lips. It had been over a decade since he'd called her that, and it was enough to make her stomach flip and legs tighten.

"Hey, Malcolm," she responded, trying to make her voice sound firm.

"Isla! Sweetie," her mom, Janet, cooed, gliding toward her daughter for a hug. "It's so good to see you. You're early this year!"

Isla hugged her mom back, nearly dropping the scones in the process.

"Here," Janet said, grabbing the box from her. "I'll take those. Sit, sit, sit. Relax. Let me get you some coffee."

Malcolm's eyes were still locked on Isla, and she blushed, the air leaving her lungs as she tried, but failed, to speak. As the warmth on her cheeks spread to her neck, she saw Malcolm's lip twitch into a smirk before he hid it behind his coffee mug. The interaction gave Isla an immediate flashback to the last time they were both here for Thanksgiving dinner. It was her freshman year at Ridge Haven University, and David had insisted on coming home with her to meet her family. The look on Malcolm's face when they'd arrived, one of hurt and betrayal, had been seared into her heart for the past decade.

"Coffee?" Another voice sounded behind Isla, and she turned to see Malcolm's gran walking out of the bathroom. "This woman's been driving for three hours; give her something a little stronger!"

Despite the tension in her heart, Isla smiled, feeling it ease ever so slightly. "Hey, Gran."

"Hey, kiddo," she said in return before wrapping her arms around Isla's back and squeezing her with the force of a thousand quilted kisses. "It's good to see you."

Isla's eyes shut, a light ray of happiness infiltrating her lungs. She'd always been like a second grandparent to her. "You too."

Gran released her grip on Isla and looked back to Janet. "I'll have a drink, too, please."

Janet rolled her eyes teasingly as she walked to the liquor cabinet. "All right, ladies, I've got wine, champagne, gin, and some eggnog in the fridge. What'll ya have?"

"Eggnog," Gran announced. "That'll be good. Start the day off right."

Isla found herself smiling again, the stress from her shoulders relaxing.

Until her eyes found Malcolm again.

"What are you guys doing here?" Isla hadn't meant to sound rude, but she feared her comment may have been based on her mother's facial expression.

"I invited them," Janet answered before anyone else could. "We always have way too much food anyway."

At that, Malcolm pushed himself off the counter, running a hand through his messy, dark waves. "Grandpa George died a few weeks ago, and your mother didn't want us to be alone today."

80

The ground shifted beneath Isla as she realized what a terrible question she'd asked.

"Oh," was all she could manage. And then, "I'm so sorry."

"Don't be," Gran said, her voice brazen. "The old bastard is getting a kick out of haunting us."

Isla raised a brow in confusion, looking to Malcolm for clarification. Instead, he smiled and shook his head, the lines around his eyes creasing ever so slightly.

How has this man aged like fine wine? Isla thought, accepting a drink from her mother.

"I'll tell you later," Malcolm mumbled, but Gran didn't miss a beat.

"I hear you two, you know."

That made Isla snicker, and for a moment, it felt like old times.

Like perhaps nothing had changed at all, and this was the way it had always been.

How different would her life be if she'd chosen Malcolm instead of David?

"You know, I think I'll have a drink, too, Janet. If you don't mind." The words tumbled out of Malcolm's mouth faster than Isla could keep up, seeing as he chose that moment to wink at her.

So different, her subconscious whispered. *So very different indeed.*

SEVERAL HOURS LATER, ISLA stood in the kitchen again, this time washing dishes. Her mom had prepared a lovely dinner, and now they were all relaxing in the living room watching *A Charlie Brown Thanksgiving*. Isla had slipped out when no one was watching so she could do the dishes as a favor for her mom.

"Hey," Malcolm said, sneaking behind her and nearly making her jump. "You wanna head out to the guest house for dessert?"

"Dessert?" Isla asked, confused. "But we already—"

She stopped dead in her tracks when she saw him rolling a familiar cream-colored paper between his fingers.

"Oh," she said simply.

He raised his eyebrows at her, a lingering question between them.

Did she want to? Yes. But should she? Honestly, she didn't know. Years ago, she would've been terrified of her family discovering that she'd smoked, but now, as a divorced business owner with no sight of children in her future, she didn't care as much about other people's opinions.

She bit her bottom lip and drew a deep breath before blurting out, "Let's go."

Malcolm smirked, and Isla threw the tea towel on the kitchen island, not caring where it landed. Together, the two of them slid on their shoes and slipped out the French doors, onto the balcony, and down the path to the guest house.

Once inside the monstrosity, Isla couldn't help the giddy feeling floating in her chest.

"I haven't done this since—"

Her voice broke off, and Malcolm raised his eyes to look at her, already catching what she'd mistakenly brought up.

"Since the summer before your freshman year of college?" he finished for her. "That sounds about right."

Isla's face reddened as embarrassment clouded her, and she nodded, not needing to say more on the matter.

"What?" Malcolm asked, continuing the conversation anyway. "No doobies in college?"

She walked into the small hallway between the bedroom and bathroom, cranking the thermostat until it turned on. "It wasn't really David's thing," she mumbled on the way back.

Malcolm smiled at her as she returned, and the sight nearly made her melt. Even after all these years, he still looked immaculate. Handsome. Gruff. He was the unkempt magazine ad parents warned about, complete with a motorcycle, messy hair, and faded tats.

And the muscles. Can't forget the muscles.

Isla averted her gaze, ignoring the heat spreading in her lower belly at the mere sight of her old . . . well, she didn't really know what to call him. They'd never officially been in a relationship, but he was so much more than just a friend.

He had been everything, while also never being anything at all. They'd loved each other as friends first, and that eventually grew into something more. Something she didn't want to face because their paths in life were so different. Isla was set to leave for college and become a career woman, while Malcolm had dropped out of school with no plans for a future. He was wild and carefree, and she was rigid and devoted. She was ashamed of herself, but when the time came and he professed his feelings for her, she took advantage of the situation, sleeping with him to fulfill an inner need she had to be desired by him, but then she told him it could never work.

Would never work.

"Should've known the accountant would be too high-strung for this stuff." Malcolm's voice fizzled through her facade, and she turned just in time to see him light the joint.

"You would be correct." David fit the bill for every stereotype you could think of when it came to an accountant.

Biting her bottom lip, she walked to the couch and folded her legs underneath her, waiting for him to pass the drug.

Malcolm followed suit, a playful expression on his face. "Here you go. Remember to inhale."

With shaky hands, she grabbed the paper, a spark of excitement sputtering in her chest.

Was she really doing this? Smoking weed with Malcolm Locklear in her mom's guest house on Thanksgiving?

Yes, she supposed she was.

She lifted the joint to her lips and took a long hit, savoring the burn.

"Fuck," she panted a second later, coughing. "I forgot how much that hurts."

Malcolm shrugged and took the joint back. "You get used to it."

Isla made an awful face before walking to the kitchen for a cup of water. "Why would you want to?" she asked after several sips.

Blowing out a line of fog, Malcolm coughed slightly. "It dulls the chaos in my mind." Then, he looked at Isla and flashed a wicked grin.

In an instant, she was transported back to that warm summer night in the backseat of her car.

Isla shuddered, remembering how marijuana made her sexual urges heighten. "That's fair," she finally said after a moment of silence.

Malcolm passed the spliff back to her as she sat back down, this time slightly closer.

She hesitated but accepted the joint, pressing it once again to her lips. "So," she said after another round of coughing fits. "What have you been up to for the last ten or so years?"

Judging by the way he looked, she assumed he wasn't single, but she did know he didn't have kids from a few choice comments his gran made at dinner. Whether that was by choice or a situation like hers, she didn't know.

He stretched his legs out on the couch, enjoying the open-concept living space. "Still working in the shop."

Isla smiled to herself, because of course that was his answer. He was always destined to take over his dad's motorcycle repair shop one day.

"I assume by working you mean running it?" she asked, sinking further into the massive sectional couch.

Malcolm cocked his head to the side. "Working, running, owning. Whatever you want to call it. It's mine, and I work my ass off for it every damn day."

Isla chuckled at the irony. "Who would've thought we'd both become business owners?" Although his path had been less conventional . . .

"And I didn't even have to go to school for it," he said, as if reading her thoughts. "Seems like the government should owe you a refund or some shit."

Isla actually snorted at that remark. "As if. I still owe them money."

"I told you it was a fucking scam." Malcolm held his hand out, indicating he wanted another hit.

Isla moved closer, handing him the joint but not making any move to return to her previous seat. "Yeah, yeah. You were right, and I was wrong." She pushed him playfully, grinning as the old, familiar sense of euphoria washed over her. And then a more sobering thought hit her.

"What about Lily?" Isla asked, referring to the girl Malcolm had dated after she'd gotten engaged to David.

"Knocked her up," he said nonchalantly, and Isla's mouth dropped open, her chest aching. The way in which some people could conceive so easily, so naturally, while she was over here killing her body, willing it to make a child out of science and dollar bills, made her skin crawl.

It took Malcolm a moment to realize his joke didn't land well. "I was just kidding, Cronkite. I haven't talked to her in years."

Tears welled in the corners of her eyes, and she didn't even bother to wipe them away when they fell. "No, it's not that. It's just . . . I've been trying to get pregnant for years with no luck."

At the sound of her own words, she felt herself go numb as a sob wracked its way through her body. Very few people knew the extent of her fertility struggles, but Malcolm was a comfort person for her, even after all these years. She felt safe talking to him.

Burying her head in her hands as another cry escaped her lips, she felt the familiar-yet-unfamiliar grip of his arms as they wrapped around her. He didn't say anything but rather just let Isla cry it out until she felt like talking. She'd always loved that about him.

"I'm sorry," she finally whispered, her face still buried into his skin.

"Don't be," he said simply. "I'm sorry for making an ass of myself."

She took a deep breath, readying herself for the conversation. "I just never thought it would be this difficult. I know so many people who got pregnant on accident or the first try, and I can't even make IVF work."

"I bet it was David's cock," Malcolm said, startling her. "Something was never right with that guy."

Isla looked up at him, her eyes wide and puffy. "I'm sorry, what?"

He shrugged. "I'm just saying. Guy was an idiot. He didn't know his ass from his head. He probably fucked something up in there unknowingly."

Isla stared at him, trying to digest his words, when Malcolm let out a laugh. "I'm kidding. Sorry, bad joke again." He paused, wiping a fallen tear from her cheek. "But that guy really was an idiot. He didn't deserve you."

The words hit Isla like a cold shower, and she sat up, Malcolm's hands sliding down her arms but not letting go.

"I should've chosen you," she said, staring into his eyes as the effects of the cannabis empowered her. "All those years ago, I was so worried about dumb stuff—things that didn't matter. But now I know, without a doubt, I should've chosen you."

Malcolm met her gaze now, his caramel-brown eyes serious, sweet, and .brooding all at the same time. She admired the way his skin had aged slightly, yet was still hardened into a facade of roughened beauty. She wished she knew what he was thinking.

Moments later, she didn't have to wonder.

Because for the second time in her life, Malcolm kissed her, and she didn't stop him.

"Holy, shit, I forgot how good sex could feel."

Isla shook out her hair, trying to smooth out the tangles in the process. Malcolm grinned at her and ran a hand through his own messy mane.

"What?" he said. "Your ex never satisfied you?"

Isla smirked. "Never like that." Their movements had been slow at first, a calm steadiness as they both tested the waters, ensuring it was what the other wanted. And then their bodies turned aggressive, possessive even, as they rocked their hips against the other, savoring the moment while it lasted.

It was incredible.

Malcolm grabbed her hand as she stood, and gently, he pulled her back down on top of him. "We could do it again," he whispered before pressing his lips against hers.

Isla knew they should be getting back. Their families were probably wondering what happened to them—not to mention she had to figure out how to get rid of the cannabis odor that was no doubt lingering in her hair.

But his lips felt good.

Too good.

She moaned as he slipped his tongue in her mouth, and she felt her body melt into his.

One more time wouldn't take too long.

She ran a hand through his hair, grabbing at the loose curls as his hands gripped around her waist. This felt so good. So fucking good. Why had she deprived herself of this all these years?

Tipping her head back to give him access to her neck, she whimpered as another wave of euphoria ignited inside of her. She was about to get up so she could rip his boxers off again, but instead, she screamed.

And not in a good way.

Malcolm startled as their bodies separated, and Isla jumped ten feet back, her gaze glued to the window above the kitchen sink.

"What's wrong?" he asked, confused.

But Isla couldn't speak because she was too stunned to voice what she'd seen.

So instead, she simply pointed, her fingers trembling.

Malcolm stood and turned, his gaze following hers.

And then he saw it, too.

Isla watched as confusion warped its way onto his face, not unlike the fear that laced hers.

There, on the window, was a message written in red:

It is the night of our dear Savior's birth!

And next to it was a bloody handprint.

REBECCA
THEN

"ISLA." REBECCA'S WORDS WERE strained, her voice frantic. "Isla, I need your help."

It was the fifth time she'd cycled between calling Isla and her midwife, and Becca cried with relief the moment her friend picked up.

"What's up, Bec? I'm at work."

A crippling pain shot through Rebecca's uterus, and she doubled over on the curb, unable to walk any farther.

"I . . . need . . . you," she tried again, still gritting through her teeth. The contractions were so close together, she didn't even know if she could make it home. "I . . . think . . . it's time."

Silence met her on the other end of the phone for a brief second, but then Isla gasped, springing into action. "Okay, I'll be right there. Where are you?"

Becca couldn't help but laugh. "I don't know. Some fucking street!" Her body ached in every fiber, every cell, every muscle. Whoever said labor felt like intense period cramps was obviously full of shit.

"Text me your location." Isla's voice came in like a steadying breath. "I'll be there as soon as I can."

Tears began to blend into her skin, but Rebecca nodded, pulling the phone from her ear and putting it on speaker as she sent a pin to Isla. "Done."

"Okay, just . . ." Isla's words trailed off, and Rebecca tried her best not to sob. "Stay warm. It says it's twelve minutes away, okay? Just hang on. I'll be right there."

The phone clicked off, and Rebecca placed both hands on her belly, trying to trick her mind into believing she was warm, her body shivering in response.

"Don't worry, little bean," she whispered under her breath. "We're going to be okay."

Another rippling pain tore through Rebecca's stomach, and she placed a hand over her mouth to keep from screaming too loudly. It was nearly nightfall by now, but still, she worried about being spotted. Someone could pull over to check on her, or worse, someone from campus could jog by. If she wanted to keep her secret safe, she'd have to move until Isla came.

Taking a deep breath, she stood again, wincing at the pain. She was still on the sidewalk and needed a place to hide. She looked around, noting the alleyways behind her. The one she'd just passed was wedged between a few run-down neighboring houses with graffiti on them, while the one up ahead was situated between an old church and a Chinese restaurant, punctuated by abandoned buildings at the end. Neither option was ideal, but in the end, she chose the abandoned buildings because, hopefully, no one would be there.

After several slow paces, she reached the corner of the block and heaved a sigh of relief when she spotted a set of stairs connected to the first complex. It looked like it had been apartments at one point in time, and Rebecca frowned, wondering why no one had taken the chance to revitalize it. Wilderby really could have been such a beautiful city if only people cared about it.

She reached the edge of the first set of stairs and gingerly sat down, trying to ignore the overwhelming fear blossoming inside of her chest.

Where's Isla? she thought as the cold from the night began to seep in. *She should be here by now.*

Wincing again, she rubbed a hand over her belly as a tear slid down her face. "It's okay, baby. We're going to be okay."

She felt the child kick in response, but it did nothing to reassure her. Something was wrong, and she knew it.

Finally, after what felt like hours, Rebecca let out a sigh of relief, crying as she saw her best friend's maroon Toyota Camry roll into a parking spot on the opposite side of the street.

"Rebecca!" Isla called, running toward her. "Oh my God. What happened?"

But Rebecca couldn't speak. Instead, a blood-curdling moan escaped her lips as another contraction began.

"Oh my gosh, oh my gosh," Isla muttered, circling around Rebecca, her eyes wide. "Okay, okay, just breathe. Just breathe." Another pause and then, "I think you might be in labor."

"No shit!" Rebecca yelled back, the worst of the pain reverberating now.

Isla didn't take offense. "Where's your midwife? Is she at the apartment? Why didn't you call her?"

Rebecca shook her head. "I tried. She didn't answer." Another sharp pain stabbed her womb, and the reality of it all came crashing over her. "I don't think we have time to even make it home. This baby is coming now." She looked at her best friend, and for a moment, it felt like they were frozen in time.

Until Isla thawed the moment with a heated reality. "We need an ambulance. Have you called them yet?"

"No," Becca bit out, her voice demanding. "Please, no. No ambulances." She'd worked too hard to keep this a secret. She couldn't give up now. "You remember the plan."

Isla raked her eyes over Becca, chewing her bottom lip as she went. After a moment, she said, "No. We're calling 911."

"Isla!" Becca yelled, desperate now. "Please, you can't." Then in a softer voice, "You promised."

"And just what the hell are we supposed to do, Bec? Deliver your baby here on the street?" She looked at her, really looked at her, and Becca almost considered her plea.

But then she shook her head, shooting her down. "No. No ambulances. No hospitals. No insurance. No documentation. No proof. No nothing!" She was rocking back and forth on the step, the cold metal making her butt go numb. "We'll just have to do this ourselves, then you can call Safe Haven for me, okay?" Becca paused and chanced a peek at Isla, who still looked uncertain. "Please, Isla. I need you."

In the dark of night, they sat in the silence together, and Becca watched Isla contemplate her request. It was ludicrous, absurd of her to ask this of her best friend, but she knew if the roles were reversed, she would do it for Isla. She prayed Isla would do the same.

"Okay," Isla finally said, breaking their trance and Becca's nerves with it. "We at least have to get you inside."

Rebecca spoke quickly now, worried Isla might change her mind if they didn't come up with a solution fast. "These buildings are vacant. They all have padlocks on them, but I don't know, you could probably break a window on one and unlock it."

Isla immediately shot her down. "Huh-uh, no way. I'm not breaking and entering. Plus, who knows who's in there. This isn't the best part of town, you know."

"Sorry, I'll try to break down and go into labor at a more convenient location for you next time," she spat back, wincing as another intense cramp unfurled in her lower back.

Isla ignored her, and Becca shoved her eyes closed, trying to think. Maybe if they could reach Isla's car, she could deliver there, but the building sensation in her abdomen told her otherwise.

They would never make it that far.

Isla's voice cut through the pain. "What about there?"

Rebecca opened her eyes, taking a deep breath. "Where?"

"There," Isla said, her voice confident. "There's a church just right there."

Despite the severity of the situation, Rebecca laughed. "I am not having a child I conceived out of wedlock inside a church on Christmas Eve night!" Her cries had turned manic, strained.

"Well, we're running out of options, Bec!"

Isla threw her hands up, and Rebecca knew she was right. Another ripple of pain wracked through her body, and she whimpered.

"Come on," Isla said, wrapping a hand around her arm and apparently not taking no for an answer. "You are not delivering this baby in the street."

Rebecca whined but didn't argue, allowing her best friend to support her weight as she prayed desperately for the health of her unborn child.

WREN
Now

"Samson, do not touch that!"

Wren swatted her three-year-old's hand away from the very breakable candles inside one of the city's local boutiques. She knew better than to bring her children shopping, but Brennan was on call for the weekend and got paged for emergency surgery, leaving her alone with the kids. Normally, that would deter her from going anywhere that wasn't a park or a family member's house, but it was Small Business Saturday, and she was determined to shop small. Not only would it support the community, but it would also impress Liam, her Secret Santa.

"Sammy, what did I just say?" She snapped at her son and grabbed his hand. "We do not touch things in here."

"Awwwwww!" Samson stomped his little foot and balled his hands into fists. "But I want to!"

Wren took a deep breath and did a quick scan of her other three children, ensuring they were still alive. "I know, honey, but we don't always get what we want in life. It's a hard lesson, I know, but everyone has to learn it. Now please, just hold Mommy's hand, and let's pick something out for her friend Liam."

Her littlest child resolved to understand but took her hand, giving Wren a minor sense of relief. It was the small victories, she supposed.

After approximately fifteen more minutes of ensuring no one snatched her kids while also listening to them fight and get into everything she told them not to, Wren caved and bought a cat mug, knowing how much Liam loved his orange tabby. She'd always teased him, saying he was destined to be an old cat dad.

Collecting her small army of children, she held the shop's door open and shuffled everyone out onto the streets and into her cream-colored mom van. She'd have to get the rest of his gifts some other time.

"Shiloh, Ava, Malachi, Samson, let's go!" She ushered the tiny humans into the back of the vehicle, a sudden chill taking over as her mind wandered back to Thanksgiving morning two days ago. "We need to hurry."

The three oldest shuffled into their seats while she attempted to wrangle the three-year-old.

"Mommy!" Samson cried. "I want to keep shopping for Liiiii-am."

"I know, honey, but Mommy's all done." She placed him in his car seat, buckled him quickly, then retreated to her spot in the driver's seat.

Here, she took a few deep breaths, drowning out the hum of her children. She loved them, of course, but every day, it got slightly harder to navigate motherhood. She'd always been destined for this role, but that didn't make it any easier. Especially when her children were fighting, like they were now. Wren sighed, and for a moment, she wondered what it would be like to be childless with no husband, traipsing the globe, just like Carley did. She saw on Carley's

Instagram this morning that she was in Guatemala again, one of her go-to travel places. Wren had scoffed at the thought, wondering what it would be like to travel there at all, much less multiple times.

"I'm hungry. Can we get lunch, Mommy?"

Ava's voice pulled Wren from her thoughts, and shame immediately flooded her. She had been blessed with this life, called to raise these tiny humans. She shouldn't think that way.

"When we get home, I'll fix you guys food, okay?"

"No, Momma, I wanna go to a restaurant!" Samson's vocabulary had certainly improved.

Ava jumped back in. "Yeah, a restaurant, Mommy!"

It would be nice not to have to cook for a change, Wren thought. She glanced at them in the rearview mirror and contemplated the thought before answering. Could her mental health handle taking four children into a restaurant alone, while pregnant, nonetheless? The thought alone exhausted her, but it would give them something to do, make the time go by faster. And they rarely went out.

Malachi gasped, clapping his hands together. "Please, please, please, Mommy!"

"Yeah, Mommy!" Shiloh begged now, too. "Please, please, pleeeeeeeease."

Wren's heart softened as she stared at her four kids, their hopeful eyes cutting through her like a honey-edged sword. "Okay," she finally said after a beat of silence. "We can go out to eat!"

Her children erupted into cheers, and she smiled, happy she could bring them this level of joy.

"All right, all right," she said, laughing with the hum of her children. "Where do you guys wanna go?"

She started the engine, ignoring the stutter as it protested. Another thing they'd have to wait for her surrogate money to fix.

"I want Mexican," Ava shouted, which instigated a series of debates, each child wanting something different.

Wren furrowed her brows, wondering what made the most sense while also being cost-effective. Her brain automatically started cataloging all the places nearby as she drowned her children out in the background. There was the Chinese restaurant around the corner, but only fifty percent of her offspring would eat that.

Next.

The plaza on the next block had a series of sit-down restaurants, but the parking situation was less than ideal for a mother with young children.

Pass.

She sighed, mentally flipping over to the fast-food restaurants on the other side of town.

"Mommy, Mommy! Look! It's your friend who wears black lipstick from all your old photos. And a boy!"

Wren's ears perked up at that. The only person Ava could be referring to was Isla, but Wren didn't know Isla was in town, and Wren certainly didn't know whether her old friend was seeing any *boys*. That would be ridiculous given Isla's mental state the last time Wren saw her. She still couldn't believe Isla had used her and David's last embryo without his knowledge.

"Where?" she asked.

"Right there!" Ava shouted, and Wren turned to see where she was pointing. "See, they're going into that building."

Wren followed her daughter's gaze, shocked when it landed on Thick Chicks.

Oh. How had she forgotten that was right there? Pregnancy brain really does get worse with each child.

When her eyes finally found Isla, her jaw dropped as she realized the "boy" with her was none other than Malcolm Locklear, the bad-boy neighbor Isla had been in love with during high school.

Suddenly, Wren had a burning curiosity for fried foods.

"Do you kids wanna go eat with Mommy's friends?"

A simultaneous "yeah" sounded from the back of the car, and Wren grinned, shutting off the engine.

Isla
Now

"What in the devil are you two doing here?" Wren hovered over their table, her giant belly and entourage of small children ever-present, reminding her again of what she'd never have.

Didn't deserve to have.

"I could ask you the same question," Isla responded, a slight annoyance in her voice.

Wren laughed. "Sweetie, I'm a pregnant mom of four who just cooked and hosted an entire holiday meal for my in-laws." She paused and threw her purse on the table. "We were due for a little Christmas shopping and a meal out with something deep-fried." Her twang and Southern hospitality were on full blast.

Assessing the situation, Isla gently scooted over in her seat, making room for Wren and her basketball team.

The world was cruel and unfair to give all the baby-making dust to one person, leaving others like herself barren out in the cold.

It's your own fault, her inner voice hissed, and she felt her body recoil like a snake.

"It's nice to see you, Wren," Malcolm said, nodding to their new table mate.

"Are you two boyfriend and girlfriend?"

Isla's eyes grew big at Ava's question.

"Ava," Wren scolded, but Malcolm just laughed.

Isla opened her mouth once, twice, thrice, then settled on, "He's a friend I grew up with."

Ava slid onto the bench beside her, nearly knocking her water over in the process. "He looks older than you."

Wren and Isla's mouths dropped open while Malcolm continued to laugh.

"I'll be sure to use some more anti-aging cream before bed, kid."

Malachi plopped down at their large, round booth. "You can't just call people old, Ava. That's rude."

"Rude!" Samson, Wren's toddler, echoed.

Isla felt a headache beginning to split down the middle of her forehead. So much for relaxing.

"Hope you don't mind us crashing," Wren said with her sing-song voice. "The kiddos saw you guys walking in and practically begged me to see you."

"That's sweet," Isla said, the words tasting insincere on her tongue. She'd seen photos of Wren's kids online, but she'd never met any of them. She wasn't sure she believed this whole thing was the children's idea.

Just then, a waitress appeared, a notepad and pen in hand.

"Oh, thank Jesus," Wren said. "I'll have your strongest mocktail, please."

Malcolm and Isla exchanged a quick glance, smiling at the server's confused face.

"Um, ma'am, our mocktails don't—"

100

Wren cut her off, raising a hand. "This baby is sitting on my sciatic nerve, and I am solo-parenting for the entire day with these goons. I really need to pretend like I'm drinking the hard stuff tonight, okay, hun?"

After scribbling down something—Isla didn't know what—the girl nodded and looked at her. "And for you, miss?"

Isla considered her question for a moment and then ordered a glass of their most popular red blend wine before Malcolm ordered a beer. While the rest of Wren's kids ordered their drinks, Isla used the opportunity to scan the room.

While she'd just been here a few weeks ago after Rebecca's funeral, she'd been too heartbroken (and drunk) to notice the establishment's features, which she now realized hadn't changed much. The restaurant bar had dark lighting throughout the entire building, Ridge Haven memorabilia on every wall, and more than a dozen TVs plastered around the bar area, making it the perfect hang-out spot on gameday. The bar itself still looked sticky and wet, but the stools had at least been upgraded to new, black vinyl compared to its previous, red-and-cracked counterpart. The nostalgia of it all hit her like the force of a sound wave.

With the waitress gone, Isla's gaze trailed back to Wren's belly, an overwhelming feeling of love and resentment blooming in her own empty stomach.

"How far along are you?" she asked.

Wren grabbed a complimentary peanut and cracked it open with her teeth. "Thirty-two weeks, but I think this girl is going to be a chunker. The doctors are talking about an early induction if she keeps measuring big, which the bio-mom is not crazy about."

Isla's heart skipped a beat. What she wouldn't do to be in her shoes . . .

"How was your holiday, Wren?" Malcolm asked, a swift shift in conversation that Isla was thankful for.

She crunched on another nutshell before answering. "Chaotic. Wild. Endearing. You know," she paused, waving her hand at the kids. "All the things you'd expect at a house full of bickering family members and loveable children."

101

She seemed to catch herself, realizing that may not be the most appropriate way to talk about her kids in front of them. "But a blessing, of course. What about you two? What are you doing here together? Isla, I didn't even know you were in town. I thought we wouldn't see you until the Secret Santa dinner."

Isla shifted in her seat, uncomfortable for more than one reason. "I came in to see my mom for Thanksgiving, and—" Suddenly, she found herself unable to articulate what she was doing here now. It wasn't the time or place to divulge what had happened at her mother's two nights ago.

"I convinced her to stay for a few more days," Malcolm finished for her. "She needed to relax. To take the edge off."

Isla shot him a look, both surprised and thankful for the path he was taking the conversation in.

As if on cue, the waitress reappeared, delivering their drinks—Wren's yellow with a cocktail umbrella sticking out of it.

"Thank you," Wren mumbled before slurping down a large drink and groaning, eyes closed. "Mmmm, that is so good."

"Not the first time I heard that today."

Isla's eyes widened at Malcolm's words, and she kicked him under the table. She hadn't wanted him to be *that* forward. "Seriously?" She tried to speak under her breath, but it was useless.

"Wait," Wren said, ignoring the still-lingering waitress. "You two hooked up?" Her voice was loud, louder than Isla would have liked.

"What does that mean, Mommy?" Shiloh asked.

Isla's cheeks flushed, and she scowled at Malcolm, who was still flashing her that boyish grin that got her into this mess in the first place.

The waitress cleared her throat, reminding everyone she was still there. "I can come back later if you're not ready to order."

Wren's gaze narrowed, but she didn't look away from Isla and Malcolm. "The children will have grilled cheeses, please. I'll take fried pickles, easy on the fried, and a bucket of fries for the table."

The girl looked jarred by the request but quickly stumbled to recover her words. "Yes, ma'am. No problem."

Once she was gone, Wren cocked an eyebrow and glared at Isla, refusing to let the conversation go. "Isla Mae Ellis, you better spill. Details, now." Her words were punctuated by the deliberate tapping of her long, clean-cut nails.

Isla blushed, looking first at Malcolm and then down at her hands, fumbling with a straw wrapper. "There's nothing to tell." She slid her gaze to the four children stuffed into the booth beside their mom. "We're just . . . two consenting adults who decided to play together."

That was one way to put it.

Malcolm nearly choked on his drink. "So transactional, Isla."

Wren snorted in unison. "Those red apples on your cheeks tell a different story, babe." She let out a dramatic sigh and took another sip of her drink. "I was wondering when you two would finally get together."

Isla's embarrassment continued to grow as she thought about their earlier encounter. The way Malcolm's lips seemed to remember all the places she liked to be touched—the way their bodies naturally melded together even after all this time.

It felt almost magical.

Until it didn't.

The sudden memory of the note on the window flashed through her mind, and Isla flinched, the movement pinching her rib cage. Her face paled, and for a moment, she felt like she couldn't breathe.

"What's wrong?" Wren asked almost immediately, never missing a beat.

Isla swiftly shook her head, throwing Malcolm a cautious glance.

"Uh uh, no, no." Wren waved her cocktail umbrella in the air. "You two don't get to keep secrets from the rest of us just because you had s-e-x. Out with it. Something is bothering you. What is it?"

It was Maclolm who spoke, his voice low as he attempted to hide the statement from the children. "Someone was watching us."

Isla's heartbeat stuttered.

Wren cocked her head to the side and twisted her brows. "So, you guys had, like, a threesome?" she whispered, covering her mouth.

Malcolm's lips twitched at that, and he nearly gagged on his drink.

"No," Isla said, answering for him. "Someone was watching from outside. And they left a note."

Wren's eyes grew wide, and she let out a breathless laugh. "Well, that's fudging creepy. Y'all gave a real-live peep show." She popped another peanut in her mouth before continuing, her Southern twang on full blast. "Probably some teen down the street."

Annoyance blossomed in the swampy pit of Isla's chest. "No. Someone's been watching me. *Stalking* me, I think."

At that, Wren finally seemed to understand. Isla waited as a different server appeared at their table, quickly dropping off everyone's food. Then, she took a deep breath and recounted the events of the previous weeks: the feeling that someone had been watching her, the note she found in the Christmas tree at work, and then finally, the message someone drew on her mom's guest house.

"I thought I was being paranoid," Isla said, picking at one of the fries and shaking her head.

Everyone says to trust your gut, but that's hard when you have one like Isla's.

Wren dusted off the crumbs from her fingers and then wiped her mouth with a napkin. "I think recent events prove otherwise." She paused, rubbing her hand over her belly, and Isla wondered what that must feel like. "Actually," she said now, her voice low, all antics subdued. "I wasn't going to say anything, but now I wonder if someone might be stalking me, too. Well, me or Scarlett. I'm not sure."

Isla's ears perked at that. "What do you mean?"

She leaned in closer, casting a quick glance at Malcolm before returning her gaze to Wren.

Her friend chewed the remaining bits of her food, not answering immediately and giving Isla cause for concern.

Isla's body felt like it was on the edge of her seat.

Probably because she actually was.

"Go on," Malcolm said, an equal amount of curiosity and annoyance lacing his voice.

Wren took a deep breath, skin prickling as she recounted how someone had smashed a window at Scarlett's house on Thanksgiving morning.

Malcolm interjected as the children dug into their grilled cheeses. "What did they throw?"

Wren's signature brow cocked again. Even when they're talking about someone potentially stalking them, Wren couldn't resist a good gossip spread, especially when the story was hers.

But Isla couldn't blame her. She was a certified Appalachian mean girl.

It was in her blood.

"Well," she whispered, "it's quite unsettling, really."

"What was it?" Isla asked so fast that the words sounded like mush.

A sly smile worked its way onto Wren's lips, obviously thrilled with her performance. "We couldn't tell at first, but then Scarlett carefully withdrew it, and once she'd cleaned it off, we saw none other than a baby Jesus ornament."

Isla's breath hitched, and she felt like she was going to vomit as Wren spoke the next few words:

"It was in a manger, covered in red paint that looked like blood."

REBECCA

THEN

"ARE YOU KIDDING ME?"

Isla banged her fists against the locked church door, sending a loud reverberation through the air. Frozen tears crusted against Becca's cheeks, her last hope of salvation gone.

"What kind of church has its doors locked on Christmas Eve?" Isla pounded on the copper frame again.

"They're probably with their families," Becca grunted through gritted teeth. "Not everyone purposely avoids spending time with their *loved ones* like I do."

She took deep, laboring breaths like her midwife taught her, a flash of anger rising at the thought. Why the hell had she taken out a student loan to pay this woman if she wasn't really at her beck and call? She was definitely getting her money back.

Lost in her thoughts, she almost missed the next instruction that came from Isla. "Come on. We'll do it here." She slipped her arm under Bec's again, pulling her down the steps and closer to the front of the church.

When they stopped, it took Rebecca a minute to understand what was happening, but when she did, her jaw dropped.

"Hell no," she said as she stared at the lifesize nativity display outside of the church.

"We're out of options," Isla countered. "Come on. It's better than the street."

"Barely!" Rebecca's voice reached a new octave as she stared at her friend in disbelief.

The idea of delivering inside the church was scary enough, but this? This was too much, too bold. Like she was trying to liken her child to Jesus or something. It felt wrong—and unnatural. She couldn't possibly have this baby in the coveted warmth of a manger scene, only to abandon it mere hours later.

So don't abandon it.

The words echoed in her thoughts, sending a chill down her spine that had nothing to do with the weather.

"I know you're the one having the baby," Isla started, her voice a jarring reality to Becca's internal debate, "but I'm the one who has to fucking deliver it and take care of your asses." She paused, grabbing Rebecca's shoulder with a firm grasp. "So buckle up, buttercup, and put your big girl panties on because your ass is about to deliver a baby inside a manger on Christmas Eve, and I really don't wanna piss anybody up there off."

Isla's eyes were locked on Rebecca's in a dead-set gaze, her harsh breath the only sound, her bunched shoulders the only movement. Rebecca swallowed as she took in her friend's words.

She was forty weeks pregnant.

Her water had already broken.

Her contractions were stifling.

The midwife was nowhere to be found.

And it was Christmas Eve, meaning the entire city was shut down.

The sudden, all-knowing thought commanded her thoughts, forcing her to take a sobering breath as she realized she was going to deliver this baby in a manger.

WREN
Now

WREN TOOK A PROMPT bite of her very fried pickle chips, letting the words soak in. Aside from Isla's fertility struggles, this was the hottest gossip she had the pleasure of dishing in months.

"A baby Jesus ornament?" Malcolm tossed another fry in his mouth and licked his fingers while she nodded. "That's gotta be connected to the messages you've been finding."

He directed his attention back at Isla, and Wren beamed, the adrenaline eating away at her.

"That's exactly what I was thinking," Wren said at the same time Isla said, "I don't know about that."

Wren pulled her home-waxed eyebrow up to her forehead. "Honey, what do you mean? Of course they're connected." One of her kids bumped her from the side, and suddenly, the high from the gossip mill started to wear off. "I've got to talk to Brennan about installing a new security system."

For a moment, they sat, pondering in their respective silence, until Malcolm finally asked, "So, who do you think it is?"

The million-dollar question.

Isla fiddled with her hair. "I don't know . . ."

Wren pursed her lips to the side, trying to gauge Isla's response. Something was *off* about her today. Her skin was always white, but right now, she looked paler than usual. Before she had a chance to ruminate on it too long, though, Malcolm spoke again.

"Do you think it was the same person who killed Rebecca?"

And just like that, a frosty chill skated across Wren's bones. "What do you mean? Rebecca wasn't murdered." She spoke quietly, her former antics set aside.

Malcolm scoffed, throwing her a side-eye before shifting his gaze back to the food in front of him. "Come on. You really think Big Time Bec died of natural causes?"

Wren opened her mouth to respond, but nothing came out.

"It . . . was a blood clot, I think," Isla finally muttered after a moment of shocked silence. "The coroner's report said subdural hematoma, which, from my understanding, is a really bad pooling of blood. There were no drugs or alcohol in her system—no signs of struggle." She hesitated now, looking to Wren for what seemed like reassurance. "Just a . . . freak accident, unfortunately."

Malcolm let out a humorless laugh. "Yeah right. You know as well as I do that girl was always destined for something like this. She settled into the wrong crowd and never grew out of it." He continued talking, all while Wren's head was spinning. "I'm willing to bet she pissed off the wrong person—probably had something to do with money. You know she didn't come from much, despite what she made herself look like to others."

Money.

Pissed off.

Wrong crowd.

The words bounced off the inner walls of Wren's mind as the theory wrapped around her brain.

"But," she started, "even if someone did . . . *kill her*, that wouldn't explain why they'd be coming after us now." She looked at the two of them wide-eyed. "I haven't done anything to make someone wanna kill me."

Malcolm did his best not to snort, which earned a strange look from Wren's youngest daughter, who was sitting next to him. "Gee, Wren, you can't think of anyone you may have pissed off in the past? Someone who may have a vengeance against you and the other prep clique members?"

She and Isla exchanged another knowing glance. They may not have been their best selves in high school, or even some of college for that matter, but they'd worked hard to move past their wrongdoings, to forget their mean girl era.

"If you're implying—"

"Oh, I'm more than implying," he said, interrupting her, and Wren braced herself for the second half of his statement. "When's the last time any of you heard from Quinn Waterbury?"

Quinn Waterbury.

The words hit Wren like a supermassive black hole, sucking her back into the vortex of her high school memories.

"At that frat party in college," Isla said somewhere in the distance. "She walked in after we'd all been drinking, but I don't think anyone spoke to her. Did you, Wren?"

Wren shook her head, but she was barely there. Her mind had hurled into the darkest depths of her soul, reminding her of exactly how cruel she'd been.

What she was capable of.

She had never meant for the joke to escalate the way it had. She'd simply been jealous of Quinn, angry at her brashness.

Isla and Malcolm continued to babble in the background, but Wren stared into her cup, seeing a younger version of herself reflected in the melted puddle of ice.

She was seventeen, a junior at East Raven High, and all she wanted was for Jones Willis to ask her out to the prom. She'd just dumped her old boyfriend, Nat Blankenship, and she just knew this was finally going to be her moment with Jones, the one she'd secretly been pining over for years.

On that particular day after class, she'd waited around the old newspaper room because she knew that's where he liked to hang out before baseball practice. She'd put on extra lipstick and straightened her hair again in the bathroom between classes preparing for him, but when she got there, she saw Quinn was already standing there, digging her nails into his forearm.

Wren wasn't stupid. She knew what kind of girl Quinn was, and she wasn't above thinking Jones would turn her down. But that didn't make it sting any less when she saw the two of them kiss a few seconds later. Anger had whipped through Wren so quickly, her body felt like it was capable of channeling lightning streaks right then and there.

But, instead, because she was too cowardly to confront either of them, she'd made up a rumor that Quinn had AIDS.

And it stuck.

Before she knew it, the rumor bloomed like an algae in a dying ecosystem. Soon, everyone in their grade knew about it, secretly making fun of Quinn behind her back for an entire school year.

It was nearly graduation by the time Quinn caught on.

"Mommy!"

A small child's voice rattled Wren from her thoughts, and she blinked rapidly.

"Yes, baby?"

Shiloh was looking at her now, her hands folded into a pleading gesture. "I said can we please, please, please have ice cream?"

Wren's heart was still fluttering from the memory. "Yes, honey. Whatever you guys want is fine."

"I just don't think Quinn would go through all this effort." Isla's voice rang in the back of Wren's head, reminding her Isla and Lover Boy were still there. "She ditched us right after high school—seemed like she made peace with the whole ordeal."

The waitress appeared, and the children promptly ordered their desserts, oblivious to the conversation.

"I don't know, ladies." Malcolm leaned back in his seat, stretching his arms and then letting one fall on Isla's shoulders. "You might want to take a hard look at your situation. She seems like the most logical candidate to me."

Wren's insides twisted at his words, her cheeks coloring red like apples.

SCARLETT
Now

"THREE . . . two . . . one."

With steady hands and one eye closed, Scarlett counted down until her finger pulled the trigger, blasting the beer bottle into a million shards. As the soundwave hit the air, a flock of birds fled from the towering oak trees. Scarlett watched as they fluttered off, wondering what it must be like to simply fly away from all their problems. To spread their wings and soar, limitless, into the sky.

After someone broke her window on Thanksgiving day, she'd decided to file a police report, despite her initial hesitations. In the end, though, it was fruitless. Silly little her thinking the cops would actually care.

She scoffed and wrapped her fingers back around the gun, thankful she'd held onto the firearm even though Calvin didn't approve. The past few weeks had remained uneventful, but she knew better than to assume she was safe. While it could've been a harmless prank, it also could've been a threat from someone in her husband's world. Being a politician automatically made them a target, and Lord knows Calvin had more than a few enemies. She had to ensure she was still a good shot, especially with her friends coming over tomorrow night.

Another loud bang sounded as she pulled the trigger again, and she smiled, wondering if Julio would be impressed.

"Mrs. Miller?"

She turned at the sound of one of her maids and saw Cora running toward her from the house.

"What?"

The woman was nearly out of breath by the time she reached her. "I'm sorry to bother you, miss, but it seems there's been an incident with your dress for the dinner party tomorrow."

Scarlett's brows furrowed. "I'm sorry, what?"

Cora pinched her face in a pained expression as a small gust of wind blew by. "They just dropped off the garment from the cleaners, steam-pressed as you like, but the painters in the front hall weren't paying attention, and well . . . "

"Spit it out, Cora," Scarlett snapped.

"One of them accidentally knocked over a can of paint all over your dress."

A shot of misplaced anger fired through Scarlett's body, and suddenly, she was all too aware of the gun in her hands.

"You mean the vintage Tiffany Monat dress with the hand-sewn emeralds I specifically picked out for this occasion?"

Cora gulped, then nodded. "Yes, I'm afraid that's the one, miss." She hung her head, making herself small. "I'm so sorry. I've already called Belinda, and she's hopping on a jet as we speak. She should be here by dinnertime with a full wardrobe for you to try on."

Scarlett wanted to scream, to rip off Cora's head and call her inadequate names, but instead, she closed her eyes and attempted to control her breathing, like the therapist had taught her.

Don't shoot the messenger.

A moment passed, and finally, Scarlett opened her eyes again to find Cora still standing with her head hung.

"Thank you, Cora." She watched as the woman looked up, her eyes widening in shock. Then, Scarlett handed her the gun and stalked toward the house. "Clean this and hide it before Senator Miller gets home tonight."

She left a speechless Cora standing on the hillside as she went inside, up the stairs, and into her bathroom.

A nice, hot shower should burn the anger away.

HOURS LATER, SCARLETT STOOD in her downstairs guest bedroom, staring at a rack of exquisite cocktail gowns.

"To be honest," her seamstress, Belinda, said, "I never actually cared for that emerald gown anyway. You'll look much better in one of these little numbers." She paused, taking in her inventory before grabbing one off the rack. "Here, try this one, darling."

Scar peeked at Julio's expression from his spot on the bed as she grabbed the item and quickly slid into it. Calvin had called after dinner, saying he'd been held up at the airport and wouldn't be home until tomorrow morning, and Julio had been more than willing to help her pick out a new gown.

Belinda's eyes had widened to large saucers when she'd first laid eyes on him. Scar wasn't entirely sure what her reaction would be, but then Belinda mimed a zip motion over her lips and said, "Mums the word, darling. He's marvelous."

Scar had bit her lip back to keep from laughing, and she thanked the universe for sending her a woman like Belinda. As the top seamstress in America, she often worked for rockstars and celebrities. Scarlett had met her backstage at a Solstice Blackwood concert once, and she knew immediately they had to work together—one of the many benefits of marrying into old money. Of course, even Calvin had complained at first, given Belinda's pricing, but Scarlett eventually talked him into it, with a little help from their sexy financial advisor.

Her husband was so stupid.

"Nope!" Belinda bellowed before Scar even had a chance to zip the dress. "That one is not right. Makes your hips look too wide." She placed a finger on her lips and then pulled another gown off the rack, this one black and long. "Here, this is much better."

Scarlett swallowed the small ache Belinda's comment had left in the pit of her stomach and instead slipped into the new gown. This one was sleeveless, had a Victorian neckline, and was skin-tight all the way to her shins. She turned so Belinda could tie the strings at the base of her neck, admiring the lacey garment in her reflection.

"This is pretty," she said, eyes dancing over the fabric and admiring how it hugged her curves.

"See," Belinda responded immediately. "I told you; this is better." She spun Scarlett back around and gathered her long, blonde hair into a high ponytail. "You wear your hair up with this. That will look best."

Scarlett nodded, then swiveled back around to check her reflection again. The garment was upscale enough for the dinner party but not overly fancy that it would make others feel informal.

It was perfect.

"What do you think, babe?" She turned again, meeting Julio's dark-brown eyes.

A small smile tugged at his lips. "You look beautiful, *princesa*."

Scarlett felt a shiver slide down her spine, nestling between her thighs. "You know I *hate* that nickname," she said teasingly, suggesting anything but.

Julio's eyes grew hungrily, possessively, at her tone. "We both know that's not—"

His words were clipped by the sudden flash of lights.

"What the hell?" Scarlett glanced at the light fixture in the room, squinting her eyes. "Did anyone else see that?"

"Trick of the light," Belinda called over her shoulder, already elbow-deep in an accessories bag. "Happens sometimes."

"Trick of the light?" Julio repeated, standing and stretching. "I don't think that's how that works, Ms. B."

Scarlett ignored their banter and waved her hands dismissively, deciding whatever it was had passed.

Until three seconds later when the lights went out.

Scarlett and Belinda screamed, and Julio cursed.

"It's okay," he said. "The power's just went out."

Instinctively, Scarlett shot out her hand, searching for his. Nestled in the tall mountains without any street lights or buzzing traffic outside in the dull night, the room was pitch black. She blinked several times in quick succession, waiting for her irises to adjust, but each time she opened her eyes, it only seemed darker.

"Ugh! Well, this is all very unnerving. What the hell is a backup generator good for if it doesn't even work?" She was beyond annoyed.

In the darkness, she felt Julio's hand clasp hers.

"Breathe, *princesa*. You're safe with me." His voice was low and gravely, protective and grounding.

Scarlett's heart squeezed as she thought about what he would've been like as a father. It almost made her feel guilty for never telling him about the baby.

She shook away the thought and opened her mouth, preparing to make a remark about the obscene amount of money they'd spent on this generator, but a woman's scream pierced the air.

Belinda.

Scarlett felt her chest heave before it fell concave against her ribcage, the old woman's cries ringing in her ears.

Dammit.

The moment she'd been waiting for.

118

Whoever the hell had broken her window had come back.

Her heart beat wildly as she contemplated what to do.

Should she run toward the sound of Belinda's cry to help? And if she did, would someone be waiting there, ready to make her scream, too?

That rationale instantly derailed her line of thinking, and she tried yanking her arm from Julio. It was too dark to see, so even if she did try to run, she'd likely trip and fall, the crash giving way to her whereabouts. That only left one option: hide.

"Let go," she hissed under her breath, ready to drop to the ground and roll under the bed.

He started to respond, but just then, the lights turned back on.

Scarlett squinted under the sudden brightness, then turned to Belinda's corner of the room.

"Belinda!"

The seamstress, who had previously been sifting through earrings and stockings and God only knew what else, was now lying on the floor, a pair of silk pantyhose tied around her mouth.

"Belinda, are you okay?" Scarlett ran to her, all previous thoughts cast aside. "Julio, help me!"

But Julio wasn't paying attention. Instead, he was stalking toward the window, mumbling something in Spanish.

"Julio!" Scarlett tried again as she yanked the cloth from Belinda's mouth and helped her sit up.

"They came through the window," he finally answered, throwing the curtains open and almost pulling the entire rod down in the process.

Scar whipped her head back just in time to see him pull his body up and through the open window. Pity and adrenaline raced through her system. She needed to ensure the seamstress was okay but desperately wanted to chase after this jackass herself.

"It's okay," Belinda wheezed. "I'm okay. Go."

119

Scarlett locked eyes with the woman, her pulse pounding beneath her skin.

"Go!" Belinda demanded this time, her throat sounding raspy. "Catch the bastard before he leaves."

Nodding, Scarlett dropped Belinda's hand, then ran to the window, fear escaping her now. In another life, she would be terrified, busy hiding out under the bed like she'd originally planned, but anger tore through her now. Not only had this scumbag busted one of her favorite windows and robbed her of several good nights' sleep, but now he'd entered her home and assaulted her seamstress. Scarlett wanted answers, and she wanted them now.

She reached the window, heart thumping, and flung her body out of it, landing on the snow-covered ground. It was dark out, but nowhere near as dark as the blackness she'd been cloaked in only moments ago. She quickly surveyed her surroundings, catching sight of faint footprints in the garden.

"Get back inside!" She nearly jumped at the sound of Julio's gravelly voice, not realizing he was only a few feet away. "It's not safe out here. You go back inside and call the cops."

Like hell, she thought.

A lot of good that'll do.

"Please, *mi reina,*" he whispered, tugging at her elbow. "For me. I would die if anything happened to you."

The taste of her nickname on his lips was sweeter than honey. The mere proclamation itself was more stunning than anything her own husband had ever done or said. And the realization made her angry.

Angry that she'd lost so much of herself in this useless marriage. Angry that she'd resorted to being someone's arm candy.

Angry that she'd cheated on a spouse.

Angry that she'd fallen in love with a man she could never really have.

Angry that she'd lost a child.

Angry that someone had violated her home.

She was the definition of a mad woman, and she needed an outlet.

"I know you're out here!" she screamed, ignoring Julio and moving past him.

No response greeted her, albeit the cold wind as it swirled by.

She took a deep breath, the rage still coursing through her veins, and started running the house's perimeter. Whoever this was, they seemed to like windows, so maybe they were hiding beneath another.

"Come out and face me like a man!"

Again, she received no response, but that only fueled her more.

She fought to adjust her vision as the last remnants of dusk settled behind the mountains, and she could barely see.

Gun, she thought. *I need my gun.*

Turning back around, Scarlett began to beeline for the other side of the house, but she wasn't looking where she was going and smacked straight into a hard chest.

"Scarlett?" Her husband's hands wrapped around her before pulling her off of him. "What are you doing?"

What am I doing? she thought. *What are you doing?*

"I, I thought you wouldn't be home until tomorrow morning." She peered over his shoulder, watching Julio sink back into the window of the guest bedroom. The sight grounded her, reminding her of how close the two men had just come to an unsolicited run-in.

"A seat opened up on my original flight." Calvin wrinkled his brow, the way he always did when he was analyzing things.

It drove Scarlett mad.

"I just . . ." she started, still trying to catch her breath while simultaneously wrapping her mind around her husband's appearance. "Never mind. It doesn't matter. Someone broke in and attacked Belinda."

Calvin jerked his chin back. "What?"

"Somebody's here! Whoever broke our window on Thanksgiving. He assaulted Belinda!" Her words were rushed, her eyes skirting back over the property.

"Honey," Calvin said, cupping her chin and tilting it up. "Have you been mixing your wine with your meds again?"

Scarlett flinched at his words, goosebumps erupting on her skin. "Excuse me?" Malice heated her gaze as she waited for him to take back what he'd said.

Calvin offered her the same polished grin he flashed for his constituents. "Oh, come on, sweetheart. You know you get a little loopy when you've had too much to drink, especially since you started taking those pills."

He was referring to her antidepressants, the ones she'd started taking after the miscarriage.

"I don't know who you think you're talking to," she sneered, "but no, I did not have too much to drink. Belinda is inside, lucky to be fucking alive, and there's a psycho out here stalking us."

Calvin tightened his gaze, turning his head toward the guest room window, then back to Scarlett. "Belinda's in there?"

"Yes," Scarlett huffed, her adrenaline crashing. "That's what I've been trying to tell you."

Why was he questioning her like this?

"Wasn't Belinda just here two weeks ago?" Calvin asked, his voice growing sterner.

Scarlett furrowed her brows. "Yes, so?"

"So am I paying her a double fee for this little visit?"

Wait, what?

Scarlett jerked away from her husband's touch, disgusted. "Calvin, who fucking cares about a price tag right now. The woman was just attacked in our home by someone who's been targeting us! What about that do you not understand?" She paused, catching her breath before adding, "Who have you pissed off enough to do something like this to us?"

She watched as his jaw flexed, and he mulled over her words.

"You're right," he said after a moment. "I'm sorry, honey. Please, let's go inside. I'll make sure Belinda's okay, and I'll make a few phone calls, take care of the intruder."

Scarlett stared at her husband, searching his face for cracks in the facade. She knew his engineered looks, his politician's gaze and how he transformed to be whatever someone needed him to be. She knew when he was being sincere and when he wasn't.

And right now, under the dark sky and in her moment of panic, she caught a glimpse of the man she once fell in love with.

If only for a moment.

"Okay," she said, breathing a sigh of relief and trusting that he would keep his word. "Thank you."

REBECCA
THEN

"DAMMIT!"

Rebecca screamed, clenching her teeth. "This fucking hurts. Way worse than period cramps!"

She was lying on a bed of hay, cradling her stomach as lightning bolts of pain lit up inside her womb. She'd watched all the YouTube videos and read all the free literature from her midwife, but none had prepared her for this.

"Fuck!" she screamed again as another ripple ran through her skin. "It's going to kill me. This baby's going to fucking kill me."

Isla pulled a blanket out of her backpack and shoved it under Rebecca. "This baby's not going to kill you," she said. "You're going to be fine."

That's easy for you to say, she thought. *There's not an infant crushing your lungs and pelvis from the inside out.*

Instead, she said, "I need something to squeeze."

Isla continued looking in her backpack before eventually turning it upside down and dumping the contents. She rummaged through the pilferage, a bead of sweat breaking out on her forehead. "Here," she finally said, tossing what looked like a loaf of bread into Rebecca's lap. "Use this."

"What the fuck is this?" she asked, picking it up and examining it.

"Sourdough."

The way she said it made Rebecca's nerves unhinged.

"I meant, why the fuck do you have bread in your backpack?" She stared at her friend, bewildered at the bizarreness of the moment.

"This girl from one of my classes gave it to me as a Christmas gift. Apparently, she makes them from scratch." Isla resumed tidying her mess before shoving a water bottle at Rebecca. "Here. Drink this."

The conversation dizzied Rebecca, but she didn't have time to ask further questions because another contraction was burying itself deep in her abdomen.

"Shit," she breathed, squeezing onto the homemade bread for dear life.

"Hey, hey." Isla's voice was calm yet commanding. "Just breathe. It's okay. We're going to get through this."

Rebecca met her gaze, her own panic reflected in Isla's irises.

"Just breathe," Isla repeated. "We're going to get through this, and then we'll call the Safe Haven helpline."

At that, Rebecca screamed as tears brimmed her eyes. She squeezed them shut, then looked away, seeing the large statues of Mary and Joseph staring at her. At first, their cold, porcelain eyes felt like they were judging her, but slowly, as the calming presence of what Becca would later identify as the Holy Spirit settled over her, the Biblical characters' serene presence morphed into something else.

She'd been so terrified this whole time of people judging her, outcasting her, but for what? So she could give her baby away to strangers with the excuse that it was better? She may not have had a perfect life, but she was also a living testament to how much a mother's love impacted her. They may not have been rich in things like her friends' families were, but they were rich in spirit.

Rich in love.

Maybe, she began to wonder, she was never meant to give up this child.

Maybe God allowed her to go into labor at this exact moment, at this exact location, to speak to her, to show her that she could do this.

That she was strong, chosen even, like Mary.

Somewhere in her forethoughts, Isla was still rambling about surrendering the baby, when suddenly, an overwhelming emotion consumed Rebecca.

"No," she blurted.

Isla looked at her, confusion evident in her gaze. "No? What do you mean no?" She sat back on her knees, giving Rebecca space to breathe as another question formed on her tongue. "Did you decide to keep it?"

Rebecca looked at her with a gaze that burned like the intensity of a thousand suns amidst the cold, midnight air. "Her," she finally said after the contraction passed. "I'm keeping her."

LIAM
NOW

8:01 A.M.

That's what time it was when Liam looked at his watch Saturday morning. He'd grimaced at the alarm clock, not wanting to get out of bed but succumbing nonetheless. It was December twenty-first, meaning he'd entered an alternate reality where he'd be visiting his hometown in West Virginia again for his friend's Secret Santa gift exchange. His flight left at noon, putting him at the Wilderby airport at two o'clock. Carley's flight was due to land at one, so the plan was for her to stick around until then so the two could meet Isla at Thick Chicks to discuss their potential Greenbrier trip. Afterward, they'd head to Scar's for the dinner party, which only slightly made the hairs on his arms raise.

He'd been cautious about going to her house instead of a restaurant, but the more he thought about it, the more it made sense. Rebecca had talked them into a sleepover after their fancy dinners out years ago, so in a way, they were honoring both parts of their tradition by having dinner at someone's house.

As long as he didn't have to slip on Christmas pajamas and stay the night at Scarlett's, Liam was fine with the change.

Groaning, he rolled out of bed and commenced his "get-ready-quick" routine, which meant he'd forego the shower, do some basic hygiene, and then style his hair quickly. When finished, he grabbed his already-packed suitcase and kissed Ben and the twins on the forehead before slipping out the door.

The trek to the airport wasn't a bad one, all things considered. Despite the chilly air, the city had a warm glow to it this time of year. Still blanketed by the dull lull of sleep, the streets hummed with caffeine, Christmas music, and fresh bagels.

He loved experiencing this version of New York.

Upon arrival, he thanked his driver and started the seamless check-in process, glad he'd arrived at the recommended two-hour wait window. Nothing was worse than being late for a flight, but being early? That was the best. He quickly went through TSA, located his terminal, then retreated to one of the many twenty-four-seven bars within the airport and ordered a spiked coffee.

Spying an empty spot in the corner, he sat down with his beverage and pulled out his phone, double-checking his message thread with Carley and Isla.

Carley: *Can't wait to see you guys! My plane should be landing around one*ish. I hope Royal's is still open. I NEED one of their biscuits!*

Liam's stomach growled at the thought of Royal's. If there was one thing he missed most about home, it was the food. Royal's, Thick Chicks, Nelson's Eats—they were all his favorite places. New York may have pizza down to a science, but West Virginia had homemade biscuits, fried bologna sandwiches, and pepperoni rolls down to a tee. His mouth watered at the thought.

Isla: *Sounds good! I'm leaving at eleven, so I should be there around two. Do you guys need me to pick you up?*

Liam hadn't even considered asking Isla for a ride. He thumbed out a quick "yes, please," then sent another text to his dad saying he didn't need to be picked up after all—a huge blessing in disguise. The less time they had to spend together, the better.

Isla: Okay, no problem. I know we're supposed to chat about our trip, but I have something else I need to talk to you guys about.

Something else? That piqued his interest.

Liam: Do tell.

Isla: I don't really wanna chat about it via text.

Liam couldn't help but roll his eyes. Isla had always been cryptic.

Carley: You're scaring us, Isla! What's up??

Isla: We'll chat soon, okay? Safe travels, y'all.

An eerie feeling settled over Liam's shoulders, making him frown. What could Isla possibly have to talk about that she didn't want to mention via text? Like, sure, they could discuss in-depth soon, but to not even mention what the topic was? That felt sus.

Very sus.

She better not be getting back together with David. Cheating prick.

Sighing, he clicked the phone shut and ordered another drink, trying to distract himself for the foreseeable future. Eventually, an employee's voice came over the speakers, informing him his plane was about to board. He finished his breakfast and returned to the terminal, ready to leave the city behind in exchange for his hometown's tall, mountainous terrain.

"FOLKS, FROM THE FLIGHT deck, we've begun our descent into Wilderby where the local time is 1:46 p.m. Conditions are good with southeast winds at five knots and a moderate temperature of forty-six degrees. We'll be arriving in about twenty minutes. Flight attendants, please prepare the cabin for arrival."

Liam blinked the sleep from his eyes, shifting in his seat as he attempted to stretch in the small vicinity. The flight had passed without any excitement, much to his liking. Things were rocky there for a second when Deborah in seat 27B started talking to him, but he'd popped his headphones in quickly, which seemed to deter her.

Upon landing, he deboarded the aircraft and followed the others as they made their way to the luggage claim. It was a small walk from the plane to the facility, but even that was enough time for him to feel the difference in the air. It was more open, more wholesome, swallowing him up like only the wilderness of the Appalachian mountains could.

While he waited for his suitcase to come out on the round conveyor belt, he pulled out his phone, checking the dozens of notifications that pinged as the airplane mode gave way to local cell phone towers. He quickly cleared the ones from social media, then tapped on Ben's name, thumbing out a quick "made it" text. His thoughts were still swimming with the ominous text Isla had sent earlier, and the more he thought about it, the more he was certain this must be about David. Isla always had a blind spot when it came to him.

Grimacing, he started to send her an individual message saying just that, but an incoming notification interrupted him.

Carley: *Actually, there's been a change of plans. I'm so sorry, guys, but I can't make it. There was a problem with my visa. Give my apologies to Scar and Wren.*

Well, that was abrupt.

Liam did a double-take, reading the message again.

Isla: *What??*

Liam: *Oh no! Is everything okay?*

Carley's response was immediate.

Carley: *Perfectly fine. Just can't make it in time. Gotta get this sorted out. So sorry, y'all!! Xoxo*

Disappointment laced its way through Liam's veins. He'd known it'd been too good to be true to assume everyone would make it. They were adults now, with busy lives and spouses and kids and businesses. Still, though. He couldn't stop his heart from malfunctioning, if only a little.

He frowned at the screen, wishing he knew a way to help. But even more so than that, he was bummed he wouldn't get to gift his Secret Santa with her presents this year.

So much for tradition.

He clicked back to Isla's name, calling her this time. "What the h-e-double-hockey-sticks is wrong with that girl?"

ISLA

Now

ISLA HATED WRAPPING PRESENTS.

There was nothing fun about it. In fact, for almost her entire adult life, she'd grown accustomed to putting things in bags, reusing old tissue paper again and again, hopeful no one would notice.

But now, as she sat on the kitchen floor, attempting to wrap Scarlett's presents by way of a social media tutorial, she cursed the idea even more.

Why did gifts have to be wrapped anyway? Who started this tradition? It was painful and annoying, most definitely not putting her in a jolly spirit.

That's not why you're upset today.

She grimaced at the thought, trying to ignore it.

Of course she was on edge. Until now, no one but her knew about Rebecca's baby. It was what had essentially blown their friend group apart all those years ago, why no one had ever done Secret Santa again. Isla had wanted to tell the others so many times, but Becca had sworn her to secrecy.

But now, with someone targeting her, Scarlett, and Wren and leaving creepy clues about that night, she knew she had to come clean soon. The story of Becca's pregnancy might be her undoing, but if what Malcolm had said was true, she had to do what she could to protect her friends, especially if Quinn was involved. Everyone knew it was only a matter of time before that girl snapped. She planned to tell Liam and Carley first while they were at Thick Chicks, then Scar and Wren at the dinner party.

They'll never understand.

But they had to, her inner voice argued.

It's not like her friends hadn't done any worse.

She swiped her finger under the line of wrapping paper, attempting to realign it so it was straight, and she cursed, a stinging sensation pricking her fingertip.

Example five-hundred-and-forty-two why Isla hated wrapping Christmas presents.

After several more expletives, she let out a long breath and stood from the kitchen floor, her body aching in ways it didn't used to. She checked the time on the microwave, nodding at the 10:00 a.m. time stamp. She needed to get on the road by eleven to pick up Liam and Carley. She cleaned up her mess on the floor and hopped in the shower for a quick body scrub before toweling off. Her bags were packed and ready to go, but she was still unsure whether she should travel in the dress she planned to wear that night or stop somewhere to change along the way.

In the end, she decided to wear it, with extra deodorant, to avoid unnecessary stops. The forecast had looked clear when she checked the weather app on her phone that morning, but that was the thing about Ohio and West Virginia: you never really knew what to expect. The weatherman could call for ten inches of snow, only for one to show up, or vice versa. The difference was that Ohio had the funds to maintain its roads better, whereas West Virginia did not. The last thing Isla wanted was to end up stranded on the side of the road in the boonies during a snowstorm, too far for anyone she knew to pick her up, forcing her to stay in a hotel or bed-and-breakfast where someone named Bill or Sally was probably way too friendly in a way that made her skin crawl.

At a quarter until eleven, Isla locked her door behind her and slid into the front seat of her car, as ready as she'd ever be for this road trip and the night's events. She was still anxious about whoever had been watching her, but also, in a weird way, she felt a sense of relief. She'd been living with this guilt and this secret for far too long, and it was high time she got it off her chest.

Sighing as she started the car, she took one last look at her reflection in the mirror. Her dark hair hung in loose curls, gently framing her face. She ran a hand through a few strands and puckered her lips before checking her teeth for lipstick stains. She was wearing her signature black shade that always made her blue eyes pop, a vibrant contrast to the hollowness of her papery pale skin.

You look like a corpse.

She didn't even shudder at the intrusive thought.

Because she agreed.

The drive itself wasn't terrible. She made good timing, considering snow started falling midway through her trip. And she'd managed to get by with only one short pit stop to use the restroom, which was likely due to too much coffee. When she turned off the highway toward Wilderby's tiny airport, she was hungry and ready for a drink.

Her phone chimed as she pulled down the holler, and although she was driving, she pulled it out and peeked at the message.

Carley: *Actually, there's been a change of plans. I'm so sorry, guys, but I can't make it. There was a problem with my visa. Give my apologies to Scar and Wren.*

Isla slammed on the brakes.

Carley was nothing if not flighty, but canceling on this of all things? That wasn't like Car.

She and Liam both responded like rapid fire, trying to get answers, but Carley's response was no more informative than her first message.

Carley: *Perfectly fine. Just can't make it in time. Gotta get this sorted out. So sorry, y'all!! Xoxo*

What the hell?

Liam must've had the same thought because her phone started immediately buzzing, his name lighting up the screen.

"What the h-e-double-hockey-sticks is wrong with that girl?" he yelled into the receiver. Isla pulled the phone from her ear, wincing. "What does she even mean there's a problem with her visa? She's *Carley*. She travels all the time. It's her career."

Isla could hear the irritation in his voice. "Yeah, I don't know." She sighed as a light dusting of snow began to cover her windshield. "Seems like this wouldn't be an issue . . . I almost don't—"

Liam continued to ramble, cutting her off. "I mean, I custom-ordered a hand-woven backpack for her. All the way from Brazil!"

His voice hit a new octave, and Isla dropped her shoulders.

"I'm sorry, friend," she said. "I didn't realize she was your Secret Santa this year."

He scoffed, a gentle hum from the airport buzzing in the background. "Yeah, so glad I spent all this money on another flight and gifts and sacrificed time with my family for her to not even show up."

Isla frowned. "That sucks. I'm so sorry." She turned on her windshield wipers and slowly put the car in drive again. "Hey, I'm almost to the airport, okay? We can still go to Thick Chicks for a little pregaming before we have to go to Scarlett's."

She hoped that would be enough to cheer him up.

A long pause awaited her.

"All right," he finally said. "I'll see you in a minute."

She hung up, her unfinished thought from earlier still lingering in her brain.

SCARLETT
NOW

THE SNOW HAD STARTED to fall harder as Scarlett stared out her window. Normally, she wouldn't be concerned, but with everyone coming for their Secret Santa party, she wanted to ensure the roads were clear enough to drive.

Especially with the visitor they had last night. Calvin had said he'd take care of it, whatever that meant, but she couldn't help still feeling a little shaken.

"The forecast says it should slow down soon," Wren said from her seat at the kitchen island. She'd arrived nearly an hour ago to help prepare the drinks. "I wouldn't worry about it."

Scar hummed in response but didn't take her eyes off the wonderland that was falling across the grounds. Their house was nudged along the backside of a rolling hill, marked by a wrought-iron gate at the bottom entrance. The road leading there was small, with only one way in and one way out. She didn't like the idea of potentially being stuck with her guests longer than she had to, but she supposed if worse came to worse, she could phone her neighbor who lived down the road and ask him to salt the holler for her. You'd think being married to a state senator would come with perks during times like this, but alas, it did not. At least not with Calvin steering the ship.

Scarlett vowed to change that once she was the one running for office.

Just then, the outline of a navy SUV came into view, and she could just make out the faint silhouette of a man and a woman in the front seat. She checked her watch and frowned, noting their late arrival.

"Looks like Liam and Isla came together." She brushed the white chiffon curtain back into place and made her way to the door, remembering she'd already dismissed her entire staff, save for the chef, for an early start to their holiday. What could she say? Several of them had kids, and she wasn't completely heartless.

Watching from the peephole, she waited until Liam and Isla were almost to the steps before she swung the door open wide with her best hostess greeting.

"Isla Mae Ellis! And Liam Renardo Walsh!" Scarlett clapped her hands together, exaggerating her Southern drawl, just like her mama had taught her. "I was starting to worry you two weren't going to show."

Scarlett believed in being punctual, and Isla was notoriously late for everything.

She sidestepped nevertheless, inviting the pair inside.

"I'm only five minutes late, Scar." Isla's voice was cold, much like Scarlett imagined her soul to be.

Liam didn't come to Isla's defense. "I wasn't driving, so you can't blame me."

Scarlett started to respond, but her words were drowned out when Isla shoved a coat in her face. "I'm surprised you're answering the door. What happened to your maids? Or are they traveling with Calvin again?"

A mixture of anger and embarrassment swirled inside Scarlett, her cheeks instantly heating. She knew the rumors about her husband, of course. Hell, she'd caught him in the act. But that didn't make it any less difficult when other people acknowledged them.

Working quickly to relax her features, she waved a hand and said, "No. I sent them home early to enjoy the holidays with their families."

Okay, so maybe her intentions weren't the purest, but her entire staff got to benefit from Scar's desire to exile their newest, youngest maid. She considered that a selfless act.

"You can set the presents under the tree in there." She pointed to the front living area, then the kitchen. "Wren is in there."

"Thanks, Scar," Liam said, grazing past her.

She couldn't help but notice he hadn't removed his shoes, and it took everything in her not to point out how rude it was to leave footprints inside someone's home. But instead, she sighed, pinching the bridge of her nose. She'd made a promise to herself to play nice tonight, because this wasn't about her. This wasn't about any of them. This was about Rebecca, and she would've wanted them to get along and have fun, to make this night as magical as possible.

A large outburst sounded from the other room as Isla and Liam made their way into the kitchen. Scarlett followed quickly after, grabbing one of Wren's drinks in the process.

"There's Mother Hen Wren and that baby belly again," Liam said, leaning in for a side hug.

"*Liam,*" she squealed. "Oh, I am so happy to see you." She finished squeezing him, then turned to Isla. "It's so good to see you again, too, babe."

Scar pinched her lips, trying not to gag at their niceties.

Everyone exchanged pleasantries for a few more moments until Wren said, "Where's Carley? When's she getting here?"

Liam and Isla exchanged a look, an ashen expression falling over their faces.

"What?" Scarlett asked, immediately picking up on what they weren't saying. "Don't tell me she canceled." The thought was preposterous. They'd been planning this night for weeks.

"She had a hold-up at the airport." Liam scratched the back of his neck, his line of sight falling to the specialty drinks on the other side of the counter. "Something with her visa I guess."

"Her visa?" Wren asked, a look of worry on her face. "So she's not coming at all?"

Isla bit her bottom lip, shaking her head. "Nope. Said to give you two her apologies." She paused, then added, "We were pretty bummed."

Scarlett curled her hands into fists several times to control her anger. "Someone probably told her there was a good deal on spliffs in the Caribbean."

"Scar," Wren warned, but Scarlett's emotions were taking over.

She'd set aside her differences with everyone in this group for one night to pay tribute to their dead friend, and Carley couldn't even be bothered to show.

"I just think it's a bit ridiculous, is all," Scarlett finally spat.

"It's not really like Carley to cancel, though." Isla's voice rose, reasserting herself in the conversation and making Scarlett pause. "I can't help thinking . . . maybe something else is going on."

Liam cleared his throat as he tipped the last of his drink back. "What, like she ditched us on purpose for her social stuff?"

Scarlett's eyes widened. "Well, did you check her social pages?"

Liam clamped his mouth shut, a confused look coating his features. "No. I'd never considered it until now."

"I didn't really either," Isla mumbled. "But it makes sense."

Scarlett rolled her eyes, snatching her phone from the counter and pulling up Carley's Instagram, then TikTok. There were no new posts, but she had the same story hovering on both platforms.

Got some exciting last-minute news! Can't share yet, but keep those notifications on! Love y'all! Xo

Scar's shoulders fell as she stared at the white text plastered against the dark screen. "I knew it."

139

She waited for the others to see what she had, and an uncomfortable silence filled the room.

"Well," Wren said, standing from her place at the kitchen island, her bowling ball of a bump front and center. "I guess it's just the four of us." She stretched her arm out, handing a drink to Isla. "But we're still going to have a great time! I spent weeks testing these recipes for y'all—with Brennan as my guinea pig, of course. Chef Sammons made all our favorite apps and is in the kitchen now baking the world's best batch of pizzas. I swear, the only thing missing is hot chocolate, Jell-O shots, and sugar cookies."

Scarlett picked up a cheese cube from the grazing table, annoyance still lacing her nerves. "Normally, I would do something a little more *je ne sais quoi*, but I wanted to keep it casual, like we used to."

She watched as Isla's eyes quickly found Liam's, then Wren's. They all exchanged a certain look and then burst into laughter, the tension in the room melting.

"What?" Scarlett did not like feeling left out.

Liam went to the refrigerator and grabbed a bottle of water. "Nothing, Scar. It's a beautiful, simple, carefully curated table of organic cheeses, fruits, nuts, and tofu. Just like the old days."

Isla snorted loudly, and Scarlett's cheeks flushed for the second time that night. "If you prefer, I could have the chef drive out to Thick Chicks and bring back that messy, garbled trash you people still eat."

Wren interjected, rubbing her hand around her belly and making Scarlett flinch. "Now, now. Down, Scar. We're just teasing a little." She grabbed a handful of grapes and popped one in her mouth. "You know your casual is fancy to the rest of us."

Scarlett pursed her lips and looked away before downing the rest of her glass. "Yes, well, it wouldn't hurt you all to take a charcuterie class once in a while."

Isla cut in now, changing the topic. "Wren, what's in this drink? It's delicious."

Wren beamed, her pregnancy glow radiating in a way that made Scarlett sick. "You like it? It's a Mistletoe Martini. It has elderflower liqueur, cranberry juice, vodka, sage, rosemary, and sugar. You know—the fixin's."

"It's stiff," Liam said, cracking his water bottle.

Scarlett's brow raised. "Speak for yourself. I added an extra splash of vodka to mine."

The ice machine in the freezer kicked on, causing a loud humming noise in the background.

"Can't please everyone, I guess." Wren returned to her spot on the stool and grabbed another handful of snacks. "Just somebody, please, drink one for me."

Isla volunteered before Scarlett could open her lips.

WREN
NOW

EXHAUSTION.

That's what rattled deep within the marrow of Wren's bones as she sat and made small talk with her friends. She knew tonight was important, and she wanted to honor Rebecca's memory, but she was just so tired, to the point where she needed one of those hand-stitched pillows that said "She believed she could, but she was tired, so she didn't." It had only been an hour since everyone arrived, and already, she was wondering how she would get through this.

A noise sounded from the back kitchen, and Scarlett clapped her hands together. "Dinner must be ready."

"Praise Jesus." Wren grabbed Liam's arm as she stood again, this time feeling slightly light-headed. If she didn't know her body better, she'd be concerned. This was exactly how she felt before going into labor with her own kids, but with this being a surrogate baby, she didn't fully trust her body. The added hormones had made this entire pregnancy different from all of her previous ones.

Chalking it up to low blood sugar, she waddled into the dining room, where Scarlett's chef was busy setting the table. "This looks fantastic! You outdid yourself."

Scarlett's face was nearly candescent. "Sammons, please tell everyone what's on the menu tonight."

Wren quickly took her seat and listened as the chef rattled off a long list of overly complicated pizzas and a simple cheese one for the "traditionalists," as he put it. Wren had already helped herself to two pieces of the lobster mac-and-cheese pie before he'd finished speaking. Normally, etiquette would require her to wait until everyone was seated, but she was hungry.

And so was this baby.

"Thank you, Chef," Scarlett said. "That'll be all. You're free to leave whenever you'd like. Thank you for staying behind the others to do this."

He bowed, thanking her and tipping his hat to the rest of the table before making a brash exit.

"I had no idea pizza could be this . . . exotic," Wren said after several bites. "I love it."

The others sat at the table, loading their plates with a variety of multicolored slices.

"You even made an alfredo one," Isla said, her voice lighter than before. "That was Rebecca's favorite."

Scarlett brushed her long, ice-white ponytail to the side, a gleam of pride in her hazel eyes. "Chicken alfredo with spinach. A classic."

"I still don't understand how y'all eat white-sauce pizzas." Liam wiped his fingers on a napkin before diving in for another cheese piece, his twang on full blast.

You can take the boy out of West Virginia, Wren thought.

"It's not even pizza," Liam continued. "It's a pie."

"Call it whatever you want," Wren moaned around a mouthful of cheese. "It's heavenly."

She heard Isla and Scarlett snicker, and for a moment, everything almost felt normal. Like it could be easy again. Like they could be *friends* again.

"I'm just happy this one has pineapple on it." Isla raised her piece in the air, admiring it before taking another bite. "I'm a pineapple-on-pizza stan."

Scarlett scrunched her brows. "You're a what?"

Wren couldn't help but laugh. Scarlett had always been a little out of touch with trends and lingo. Honestly, Wren only kept up with it now because she heard her children say it, and she had to know what it meant. She started to interject to say as much, but just then, her phone vibrated. Wiping off her hands so as not to leave grease stains on the screen, she picked up the device and saw her husband's name.

Brennan: *Did you see the forecast update?*

Wren swiped out of the app, tapping on her weather one and groaning when she saw it.

Scarlett was quick to notice. "What's wrong?"

"There's a winter storm advisory. It was supposed to clear up by seven when I checked earlier, but now it's saying it'll go through until morning." She paused, pulling up the local news channel's social media page, and her eyes widened. "They're calling for eight to ten inches of snow."

"Of course they are," Isla mumbled. "That's gonna be fun driving home tomorrow morning."

Wren considered this, wondering how Isla's car would survive a three-hour drive in these conditions. Before she could get out another thought, though, her phone lit up again, only this time, Brennan was calling.

She answered quickly, her voice low, not wanting to be rude but not wanting to get up. "Hey, babe, what's up? We're eating dinner."

"Did you see my text?" His voice was laced with concern.

"Yes," Wren said, exasperated. "Lots of snow. I'll be sure to be careful coming home."

"No," her husband said, speaking faster, more urgently this time. "I sent a second one right after. There was a wreck on Route 52. Honey, they've closed the roads."

Dread pooled in the pit of her stomach, just beneath her surro-child's tiny left foot.

"What do you mean?"

Brennan let out a breath. "I mean, there's no way you can come home tonight. I was already on the fence about you driving due to it not being safe, but now they've physically closed the main road that leads to Scarlett's, meaning there's no way for you to get here."

Scarlett and Isla were staring at Wren now, noticing something was wrong.

"Well, that's simply not going to work," she said, voice unsteady. "I'll just take the back way, around the hill."

"Absolutely not," Brennan demanded. "It's far too dangerous. You're going to have to stay the night there, honey. All your friends will. I just wanted to call and check in to see how you were feeling and if the baby's okay?"

Wren's head swam with this information. It's not that she minded staying at Scarlett's, but the idea of being isolated from the rest of the world when she was thirty-six weeks pregnant with someone else's child made her uneasy.

"What's wrong?" Scarlett could read her like a book.

When Wren didn't answer right away, Liam seemed to finally catch on that something was up. "Wren?" he asked.

She let out a deep breath, her shoulders slumping in the process. "Brennan says there's been an accident. They've shut down the main road, the one that connects your holler, so there's no way for any of us to get home." She felt the baby kick, and she instinctively placed a hand there, wanting to feel its presence. "We're stuck here for the night."

Wren watched as, one by one, her friends exchanged glances, understanding registering on their faces.

"Shit." Liam's voice startled Wren. "I should've known something like this would happen."

"This is silly," Scarlett said, sitting straighter in her chair—if that were even possible. "Surely there's an alternative route y'all can take."

Wren shook her head, acutely aware Brennan was still on the phone, listening. "He says it's too dangerous. The only other way is around the backside of the mountain, and even that dumps out on 52." Brennan blurted something about impacted snow and black ice in her ear, which she reiterated to the group. "We are stuck here until they reopen the main road."

"But," Isla started, pushing herself back from the table. "But that could be days."

She wasn't wrong. Route 52 would likely be cleared tomorrow afternoon, but no one would come around these parts to clear the holler roads for three or four days. Scar's neighbor could salt it, but if this storm was anything like what they were predicting, then it wouldn't do much good. They'd have to wait for someone to come dig them out.

Scarlett mumbled something incoherent under her breath, then raised a hand, apparently wielding the conversation in another direction. "It's fine, I guess. You can all stay here. We have a generator—"

Her voice broke off, causing everyone to look over.

"It's fine. We'll be fine."

Something about her statement didn't fully reassure Wren. "What if something happens? Like to the baby?"

"Relax." Scarlett waved a hand and returned to eating her food (with a fork and knife, she might add). "Nothing's going to happen. Like I said, we have a backup generator in case the power goes out, and we have food for weeks. You and the baby are safe here and gonna be just fine."

146

Wren's eyes fell down to her nails, where she'd been picking at her chipped polish. Could she really stay here with these people? Be trapped with them?

But then again, what choice did she have? She could barely drive well on dry roads, let alone an icy one in worsening conditions. What would she do, slip and slide her way to the end of Scarlett's road and then beg the police officers to let her sneak onto the pavement?

Sighing, she cleared her throat and said goodbye to her husband, assuring him everything would be fine. When she looked up, all eyes were on her.

"Well, Scarlett, I hope you have some pajamas that will fit me because I am not sleeping in this outfit. In fact," she added, pausing, "I would like to go ahead and get changed now, please. If we're staying in for Lord knows how long, I want to be comfy."

LIAM
Now

WEARING ANOTHER MAN'S FLANNEL pajamas was not part of Liam's plans tonight.

In fact, it was the exact opposite of what he'd hoped for, like somewhere deep in the recesses of his mind, he knew he was destined for this.

They were all destined for this.

He sighed, looking down at Calvin's baggy fleece pants.

Such a hetero choice.

He snapped a quick photo to send to Ben, angry that he'd forgotten his own pajamas when packing, and then shoved his phone in the flimsy pocket before returning to the living room with the others. When Wren had announced she wanted to be comfortable for the night, everyone else followed suit, borrowing clothes from Scarlett and her husband's closet, unbeknownst to the senator, of course, who was away on business.

Per usual.

"I feel like I've stepped into a time warp," he said, settling into the corner seat of the tan microfiber sectional. "Is Robin Thicke going to sing about blurred lines while we cram for a math final?"

Isla snickered from her spot on the floor where she'd been nursing another cocktail, then twisted her lips into an evil grin. "I know you want it."

Liam couldn't help but roll his eyes as she continued with the next line. He was about to jump in and sing with her, but Scarlett's voice cut through Isla's like a knife.

"That song is disgusting. You know it promotes rape culture."

Liam tucked in his lips as he watched Isla restrain her features. The two had always gone at it regarding issues like this. Liam often thought of them like oil and water, wondering how their friendship had lasted as long as it did.

Instead of responding, Isla tipped back the rest of her drink and stood. "I think I need another *Mistletoe Martini.*" She said it with an edge to her voice.

"Grab me one, too, please," Liam called after her.

It was a wonder none of them were alcoholics.

Moments later, Isla returned to the living room, this time sitting on the sofa beside Liam.

"Okay," Scarlett's voice rang, her earlier frustration seemingly dismantled. "Time to open presents and see who everyone's Secret Santa is this year."

Although Liam was sad about the way Carley canceled and his Secret Santa not being here, he felt a prickle of anxiety and excitement lace its way through his chest. He always enjoyed this tradition. Rebecca would've been so honored if she could see them now.

He turned his attention to the massive Christmas tree that enveloped the room. It must've been at least fifteen feet, he guestimated. Tall enough to hide all their secrets. Maybe bury a body.

He smirked at the odd thought, pushing it aside, ready to enjoy the rest of their estranged night.

"I'm so excited." Wren sat in the oversized chair near the fireplace, her legs stretched out before her. Liam wondered how long it would be until she fell asleep.

"Now," Scarlett said, walking over to the tree and retrieving a brown package from the large stack of objects. "Who wants to go first?"

Silence filled the room for a beat before Isla asked, "Well, whose name is on the package? Whoever it is, they can go first."

Scar's eyes flitted down to the brown paper box as everyone else waited for her answer. Liam watched as she flipped it around, her face twisting as she searched for the name tag. "It doesn't say."

Eyes darted around the room as everyone waited to see who would fess up to it, but after it was clear no one was going to claim it, Scarlett said, "Never mind. This must be one Calvin got me." She sat it to the side and picked up another package wrapped eerily similar. "Okay, this one is for . . ."

Liam waited, a twinge of nostalgia weighing on his chest despite the awkwardness in the room.

"No one," Scarlett said under her breath, her face still twisted in confusion. "This one doesn't have a name either." She looked up, and now, Liam saw red splotches forming on her porcelain cheeks. "Who wrapped these? And why didn't you put a name on them? Honestly, it's very annoying."

But once again, silence filled the air.

Isla looked at Liam, who shook his head and then shrugged. "Wasn't me."

"Me neither," Isla said.

Scarlett let out an annoyed breath. "Okay, then it must have been Wren." She turned to her left, where Wren was now dozing.

Called it, Liam thought.

He and Isla laughed, but Scarlett seemed even more annoyed at this point. "Wren!" she yelled.

Wren's eyes popped open, and she lurched forward in her seat. "What's wrong?"

Poor woman, Liam thought.

"You fell asleep," Scarlett said, brushing a loose strand of hair from her face. "I was asking who wrapped these presents. It wasn't us, so it must've been you." She shifted back and forth on her feet, and Liam recognized it as her telltale sign that she was trying not to scream.

"Oh, sorry," Wren's sheepish voice came out barely above a whisper. "This baby's draining me." She paused, wiping what looked like drool from her face before squinting her eyes at the package. "Nope," she said after a moment. "That's not from me."

Scarlett's body began to twitch in overdrive. "What do you mean it's not from you?"

Wren openly rolled her eyes and then laid back against the cushion. "Just what I said—it's not from me. Mine are wrapped in cats wearing ugly Christmas sweaters."

Liam's mind wandered back to Carley. "Did Carley send them somehow?"

"No," Scar answered almost immediately. "I just had new security cameras installed, and there were no delivery trucks outside today. Come to think of it . . ." She paused, walking into the other room and retrieving something similar to Liam and Ben's baby monitor. "I don't think our regular mailman came today either."

"Wait," Isla said, cutting in as Scar scrolled through footage. "So if we didn't put those under the tree, then who did?" Her question was directed at the entire group, but all eyes turned to Scarlett for an answer.

It took a moment for her to understand, but then shock registered on her face. "What? You think I did this?"

Liam looked at Isla, who raised her brows and shrugged her shoulders. "I'm just saying," she continued. "None of us put those presents under the tree, and this is *your* house. And let's not pretend you're above playing some elaborate prank on us."

Scarlett's mouth dropped open. "Excuse me, but I did no such thing. No offense to whoever's lying about this, but I would never wrap my gifts in something as ordinary as plain brown paper." She paused, setting the second gift aside and pilfering through a few more. "I wrapped these, for Isla," she said, tossing icy blue packages at her. "Merry Christmas, *friend*."

Her attempt at a joke fell on deaf ears as Isla caught the package and set it to the side.

"Okay, but seriously," Scarlett said, more agitated than ever. "Who are these gifts from? There's, like, ten of them."

Liam stood at this comment, counting the beige packages. "You're so dramatic," he said, whipping around. "There are four, not ten."

Another thought occurred to him, hitting him like a lightning bolt to the chest.

One for each of them.

"There are four," he reiterated, his voice dropping. "They knew Carley wouldn't be here."

"What?" Scarlett asked, her voice demanding.

Liam turned back to face her. "There are only four packages. Carley was supposed to be here tonight, so that means, whoever these are from, they knew she wouldn't be here."

"How do we know they're for us, though?" Wren asked, speaking up for the first time since the debacle started.

Scarlett's foot must've been on fire from the rate it was tapping. "I already told you, I would never wrap my presents like that."

Her voice was snappy, but Wren didn't seem offended. "Yes, but there are other people who live here, Scar. Your husband, the maids, the chef . . ." Her voice trailed off, and she waved a hand in the air. "Maybe one of them put them under the tree before leaving today."

Scarlett opened her mouth, but for once, she appeared speechless.

After a beat of silence, Liam cleared his throat and spoke up. "Well, there's only one way to find out." He felt everyone's gaze on him, but no one said anything.

And then he made the most obvious suggestion:

"We could open them."

PART II

REBECCA

THEN

"IT'S A GIRL?" ISLA asked, her voice suddenly gentle.

Rebecca bit her lip to keep from crying more than she already was. "It's a girl." Another contraction broke her back, sending warning bells off.

Isla must've noticed the alarmed look in her eyes because she said, "What's wrong?"

Rebecca suddenly had the unrelenting urge to shit.

"I think it's time to push," she said, keeping her initial thought to herself.

Isla locked eyes with her, and together, they nodded. All around them, snow continued to fall, blanketing them with an ethereal glow. Becca nearly laughed at the irony of it all as the nativity scene characters continued to stare at her, but for the first time in a long time, she felt like her faith was being restored. No longer was she worried about the judgments of others or the compulsive need to fit in.

Because there, in that odd little pocket of time and space, Rebecca was becoming a mom.

And she was damn proud of it.

"You can do this," Isla said, rolling her sleeves up and dousing her hands in hand sanitizer.

Rebecca took a deep breath in through her nose and let it out with her mouth, nodding but unable to speak. She prayed Isla would take over and understand what was happening, what she needed, because despite the pain she'd felt before and the unending yelling she'd seen in the movies, there was no fucking way she was going to be able to speak, let alone scream while trying to push this baby out. It was going to take every fiber, every ounce of her strength to deliver this child.

Thankfully, Isla picked up on the silence as her cue to step in, and she helped tug her friend's leggings and panties the remainder of the way off before draping a small blanket over her legs. Rebecca had never been the type to care about her friends seeing her naked, but she cringed at the thought of her best friend simply staring at her vagina now that it was go time.

How long had it been since she'd shaved?

Ugh, so not important right now, Bec!

She started to make a joke about it as the pain subsided, but almost immediately after, another contraction took over her lower half, and she grabbed her loaf of bread and held onto it for dear life.

"Okay," Isla said, her voice rising in pitch. "Push, Becca! Push!"

ISLA
NOW

WHAT WAS IN THOSE boxes?

And who were they from?

Isla's heart raced as she stared at the brown parcels, her mind catapulting to the worst-case scenario.

You know who it is.

Quinn.

But how? If it was really her, how could Quinn have known they'd all be here tonight and that Carley wouldn't?

Even more importantly, how did Quinn know about Rebecca's baby?

Dammit.

Isla had been so rattled by Carley's sudden departure that she lost the nerve to tell Liam about Becca's pregnancy. The thoughts had echoed around in her head the whole way to Scarlett's, but she couldn't bring herself to say anything, couldn't figure out how to broach the topic when such an eerie feeling had already surrounded them.

Now, she realized, she may not have a chance to come clean.

Because she had a sneaking suspicion these boxes might just expose her.

"Oh, for Heaven's sake," Scarlett said, not wanting to take Liam's advice. "One of you had to have done this. Stop lying."

Her voice rose with anger, but Wren responded for the group, unbothered by Scar's theatrics.

"Please," she said, "save us the monologue." She waddled to the tree and scooped up the boxes, swiftly handing one to each of the others. "Here, let's just open these and settle it once and for all so we can move on with the night. I still want to know who my Secret Santa is. It's the first year I haven't figured it out beforehand."

Wren continued to ramble in the background, but Isla wasn't paying attention. She was too consumed by the weight of the package in her hands. Not that it was physically heavy, but emotionally, she feared whoever had been watching her was about to blow up her entire world.

Again.

The sound of tearing paper finally startled Isla back to the present, and she blinked quickly, trying to clear her thoughts. Then, slowly, she lifted a finger and ran it across the beige seam, separating it from the piece of tape that had been holding it down.

Here goes nothing, she thought.

Heart beating faster, she sliced through the rest of the paper with the tip of her stiletto nails, and she froze when she saw the box.

It wasn't anything exciting—just a plain brown box to match the plain brown paper and dainty bow, but she knew, deep in her gut, that just below the cardboard's surface, lay something sinister.

Something restless.

With a deep breath, she grabbed both sides of the lid and yanked it off, the sound of gasps filling her ears as the others opened theirs.

What the fuck?

Her eyes widened, and her breathing hitched.

"What kind of sick humor is this?" someone said in the background as another scream permeated the air.

Isla looked up momentarily in an attempt to gauge her friends' reactions, but then her eyes fell back to the contents of her box.

Because lying inside was a pile of scattered teeth.

Human teeth.

And they were drenched in blood.

Panic rose in her throat as her body threatened to scream again. What the fuck was this? Who had done this? And whose fucking teeth was she looking at? It was one thing to leave threatening messages and follow her around, but this? This was truly terrifying.

It chilled Isla's blood to the core.

"I'm gonna be sick," Wren said. "Oh, fuck."

Isla looked up again, noticing the urgency in her pregnant friend's voice, and watched as Wren dumped out the contents of her box before proceeding to throw up in it.

The sound and scent of vomit made her own stomach roil, but beyond that was an increasing, perplexing curiosity to know what Wren had just dumped out.

Because it didn't look like teeth.

"What was in your box?" Isla asked, voice unsteady. Her eyes were locked on Wren, but she could feel the others watching.

Wren took a cloth napkin from the coffee table and dabbed her mouth, then her forehead before returning Isla's gaze. "A finger," she finally said after a moment, and then, "I think I'm going to be sick again."

Isla cringed, preparing herself for the sound of more vomit, but Wren stood and waddled to the bathroom, giving them all one small sense of relief. Isla's eyes searched the ground now, pausing when they landed on the severed phalange.

"Mine are toenails," Liam said, an air of disgust in his voice. Isla snapped her attention to him as his voice continued to rise. "I thought it was a gross prank, but that's someone's fucking bloody finger on your carpet!"

This was so much worse than Isla thought.

"Mine are teeth," she whispered, voice barely audible as she stared back down at the now open box.

"What the fuck," Liam breathed.

Suddenly, the sound of someone clearing their throat seemed to break the spell, and they both looked at Scarlett, who'd been quiet until now. "Mine is full of hair—*red* hair."

REBECCA
THEN

REBECCA'S AMBER-RED HAIR WAS drenched in sweat, despite the freezing temperatures.

"I can see her head, Bec!" Isla said, her words turning to fog in the December air. "Just one more push! Come on, you can do this."

But Rebecca didn't know if she could do this. She'd been pushing for God knows how long, all with little to no success. At one point, she thought the baby was going to come out, but then her little head slithered back inside, and Rebecca cried.

"Come on, Bec," Isla said, trying again. "Just give me one more big push. She's right there. We can do this. She just needs her mommy to do one more big push."

It was dark and cold and wet everywhere she looked, but at those words, Rebecca took a deep breath and barreled down with the lower half of her body, pushing with all her might. The pain was electric, a terrifying sensation as her body endured the ultimate ring of fire, and for a moment, Rebecca thought she might pass out.

But she didn't.

By the grace of God and this damn nativity scene, Rebecca birthed her beautiful baby girl into the world during the next push.

"She's here!" Isla's face lit up with joy as the church's bell tower tolled, signaling midnight, and Rebecca threw her head back in laughter, a sense of great relief washing over her.

She'd done it.

Despite all odds, she'd given birth to this beautiful child at the stroke of midnight on Christmas Eve in a manger, and they'd both survived.

Or so she thought.

After more than a moment had passed and Isla hadn't given her the baby, she lifted her now-weak head. "Give her to me," she said, breathless. "Give me my baby, Isla."

But Isla wasn't responding.

Instead, she was staring at the child, a blank expression on her face.

Suddenly, the pit in Rebecca's stomach grew. "Isla," she shifted her weight until she was leaning up on the palms of her hands. "Give me the baby. Give me Poppy."

At the sound of her daughter's name, Isla looked up, and Rebecca's chest cracked as she realized what was wrong.

Her daughter wasn't crying.

Scarlett
Now

She was going to be sick, just like Wren.

Perhaps worse than Wren.

"There's no way," Liam said, now sitting again, his hands limp at his sides.

There, coiled at the bottom of Scar's box, was a large bunch of wavy, copper-colored hair—the exact same shade as Rebecca's.

"Let me see." Scarlett looked up, blinking from her trance at Isla's words. Her hand was outstretched, reaching for the box.

Bewildered, Scar offered it to Isla, her thoughts an obliterated mess.

How was this possible? How had someone done this? *Why* had someone done this? Of all the things that could've gone wrong tonight, she did not imagine *this*.

Isla made a garbled sound, quickly pushing the box back into Scarlett's hands before pacing toward the window.

"I don't understand." Liam's voice cut through the tension in the room. "Why would someone send us this?"

Isla continued to stare out the window, and the view triggered an unwanted thought for Scarlett.

The intruder.

What if Calvin hadn't taken care of it? What if whoever had broken in last night was back again?

What if they left the presents?

No, she told herself. No, it can't be.

She refused to believe that. Her husband may be a certified liar, but one thing he would not do is risk a publicity scandal. He would've made the calls, done whatever means necessary to ensure this person didn't come back, not for their safety, but for their reputation.

His reputation.

Whatever was happening here must be something else, a cruel prank gone wrong perhaps.

She cleared her throat, presenting a new option. "Well, I, for one, don't think this is very funny."

Isla swiveled her entire body around, concern etched in her face. "What do you mean?"

"Well," she started, mulling over the thought as she strengthened the theory. "One of you clearly bought out the Halloween store, or something crazy, and snuck these boxes in here as a cruel joke, but I don't find it very funny." She huffed out a breath and smoothed the invisible wrinkles on her pajamas. "It's in poor taste, honestly, and I don't appreciate it. And to think, I offered to host this lame-ass party in my house."

Isla's mouth dropped open, causing Scarlett's confidence in her new-found rationale to falter, if ever so slightly.

"You've got to be fucking kidding me," Isla spat, crossing her arms. "We get chopped-up bits of our dead best friend during our Secret Santa tradition, and you think one of us did this as a *joke*?"

"Do we really know it's her, though?" Liam interjected.

"Who else would it be?" Isla asked pointedly.

"I don't know," he replied, scratching his head. "I just don't understand . . . any of this."

Scarlett's nostrils flared as she listened to them go back and forth. It had to be a joke. It just had to. There was no way someone actually did *this*. Unless . . .

A large belch erupted from the doorway as Wren walked back in. "Sorry, excuse me," she said, covering her mouth. "Did you all . . . pick up the . . ." Her voice trailed off as she attempted to hold back another burp, unsuccessfully.

Scarlett's gaze snapped back to the dismembered finger lying on her floor, and she screamed for her maid before remembering she'd sent them all home. "Dammit, why did I give them the night off?"

"Here, I'll do it," Isla said, giving her a nasty scowl as she bent down to scoop up the digit with the hem of her sleeve. "Here," she said to Liam this time. "Hand me the box, please."

Liam shuffled his feet against the hardwood flooring, obeying her command, and Scarlett watched in horror as Isla dumped the bloody finger into the box.

"We need to call the police," Wren said, still covering her mouth. "This has to be whoever's been stalking you, Isla—and whoever threw that sweet baby Jesus through your window, Scar!"

Scarlett's brain did a rewind.

"Wait a minute," she said, raising a hand. "What did you just say? Has someone been stalking you, Isla?" Her heart was beating wildly now. She didn't want to believe it.

Isla had returned to pacing, but Scar noticed she was biting her lip.

"Yes," Isla said, hesitation lining her voice. "Or I don't know. I think so." She paused, blowing out a breath and placing her hands on her knees as she bent forward. "I had a few instances where I felt like someone was following me, but I shrugged it off, thinking I was being paranoid. Then someone left a note at the coffee shop one night after work. It was a lyric to an old Christmas hymn. And then when I was in town for Thanksgiving, someone left another message on my mother's window, letting me know they'd been watching me."

"The guesthouse window," Wren added, clarifying. "Where she and Malcolm were doing the . . . you know." She raised her brows, indicating something intimate and causing Scarlett's eyes to grow even wider.

"Wait, Wren, you knew about this?" She was baffled that her best friend hadn't told her.

She nodded rapidly. "Yeah, I saw them together at Thick Chicks. Did I not tell you? I thought for sure I did."

Scar's frustration only grew. "No, you most certainly did not! It would've been nice to know someone was stalking one of us before I invited you all into my home, where we're now trapped in the middle of a snowstorm with fucking pieces of a human body!" She was heaving by the end of her monologue, fear finally lacing its way around her, coiling at the base of her spine.

Wren's puppy dog face looked wounded. "I'm—sorry," she stammered. "I thought I had." She took a deep breath, then sat on the edge of the sofa. "This damn pregnancy brain is killing me."

Oh, for fuck's sake.

This could not be happening. The notes, the watching, the ornament, the invasion, and now these fucking boxes. Scarlett could no longer ignore the growing pit in her stomach that said these were all connected.

Someone had been targeting them.

But the question remains, how did they do it?

How did they stuff pieces of Rebecca under her Christmas tree without her knowing?

She sank to the couch as her mind reeled, combing through the logistics. Rebecca had died over a month ago. They had her funeral at that blasted Catholic church in the middle of town and then buried her the next day. Someone would've had to dig her body up, chop off a few pieces, return her to the grave, then sneak the boxes into the house without being noticed. It was impossible.

And yet, here she stood, surrounded by the ghosts of her friends' past as Rebecca's body parts lay wrapped in Christmas gifts for them—their Secret Santa from beyond the grave.

Liam cleared his throat, pulling her from her spiral. "Do you guys think . . . Carley had anything to do with this?"

A sudden chill hit Scarlett as she locked eyes with the others.

"What, like you think she was behind this? That she's pranking us for her social media following? A new segment called *Fuck With My Friends*?" The idea infuriated Scarlett.

"I don't know," Liam countered. "Maybe? I mean, she canceled at the last minute and low-key lied to us about it. I feel like we can't rule it out."

"Or it could be Quinn." Isla's voice was so low, Scarlett was sure she'd misheard.

"What are you talking about?" she asked.

But Isla didn't respond. Instead, she gazed at Wren, who was shaking her head and staring at the ground. "No," Wren said. "No, it couldn't be. What we—I—did wasn't kind, but she wouldn't go murdering Bec and then terrorizing the rest of us because of a stupid rumor. I refuse to believe it."

"Murder?" Scar's voice reached a new octave. "What are you talking about *murder*?"

Wren went stone silent.

"Malcolm thinks someone murdered Rebecca and framed it as a freak accident. He thinks whoever it was is probably the same person who's messing with us now." Isla blurted the words with a pained expression on her face.

Liam's theatrical gasp hit the height of Scar's twelve-foot ceilings, making her temples wince.

This was all too much.

Too chaotic.

Too irrational.

Too unwanted.

She needed to lie down.

"We just need to call the police and stay calm," Wren said, her mothering instincts taking over.

Scarlett would be annoyed if she weren't grateful for her calming nature right now. She chewed over the thought for a moment, remembering how useless the cops had been when she filed her police report last month. After that, she'd vowed never to rely on them again, but apparently, she couldn't rely on Calvin either, seeing as he had *not* taken care of whoever the hell this was, leaving them exposed to real fucking danger.

"Fine," Scarlett said, throwing up her arms. "I'll call them." She mumbled something else inaudible under her breath as she took her cell phone out of her pajama pants, and then her eyes went wide.

No.

"You've got to be fucking kidding me."

That got everyone's attention.

"What's wrong?" Isla asked.

But Scarlett didn't answer right away. Instead, she held up a finger and then walked off to the side by the Christmas tree, trying to make a phone call.

"Dammit!" she said after a beat of silence before turning back around to face the group. "I don't have service."

Liam actually laughed at that, although it was devoid of humor. "Of course you don't." He shook his head and pulled his own device out of his pocket, a delirious look on his face.

Scarlett's anger dissipated as their new reality sunk in. "What about you? Do you have service, Liam?"

Another laugh told her everything she needed to know.

She quickly looked at Wren, then Isla, both of whom turned their phones to her, revealing the same fate:

No Service.

LIAM

NOW

THEY WERE ALL GOING to die.

That's it; he knew it. Not only was this how every horror movie started just before they unalived someone, but it was also *Liam* and his fucking *curse*.

Dead mom?

Check.

Dead brother?

Check.

Dead grandma?

Check.

Dead friend?

You guessed it: check.

It was only a matter of time before the fucking Grim Reaper came for him, too.

He needed oxygen—lots of it. Like a full-fledged *brace-for-impact-we're-crashing* level of oxygen.

Breathe, Liam, Ben cooed in his thoughts.

His eyes popped back open. "Ohmygosh, Ben! The kids!" Everyone turned to him, confused. "How will they manage without me? I work for a startup company; I don't have fucking life insurance!" His eyes danced around the room as the panic set in. "I can't leave them without my income. Ben is a *teacher*, for crying out loud."

Wren placed a hand on his lower arm from her spot on the couch. "Don't panic yet, honey. I'm sure it's going to be okay. Scarlett, you always have service here. Surely this is a mistake—a glitch from the storm."

Liam wanted to cackle at Mother Hen Wren's last-ditch effort to comfort them.

"I . . . I don't know," Scarlett finally said after a beat of silence. "I mean . . ." She stared at the ground, apparently in a state of shock. "I used to have spotty service years ago when Calvin and I first moved here, but he had boosters installed." She paused again, the color draining from her already ashen face. "They must've stopped working."

Or someone cut them, Liam's inner voice whispered.

And then he said those same words out loud, no longer having control over his normally cool exterior.

"Nobody cut them," Scarlett snapped, seeming to regain some sense of self. "That would mean—"

"That someone's still here," Isla breathed, cutting in.

It took a moment for the group to process what she was saying, but once it did, the words lingered in the air, forcing everyone to confront this possibility, this truth, despite no one wanting to lay claim to it.

Liam surely fucking didn't.

His thoughts returned back to his family and the way Ben had warned him about coming. His husband would be extra pissed at him if he died because he ignored his advice.

Liam had to get out of here.

"I shouldn't have come," he said, a new idea springing to the forefront of his mind. This was all a big mistake, and he'd let them fool him into thinking otherwise. "I'm leaving."

"But Liam—" Isla started.

"The roads!" Wren cried.

Objections flew from every corner as everyone tried to convince him to stay, but he didn't care. He needed to get the fuck out of this place before death moved past Scarlett's doorstep and into the house.

"I'd rather risk the roads than be stuck here like a sitting duck," he said, attempting to quiet the objections as he made his way to the front door through the maze that was Scarlett's house.

"Please, we should at least wait for the police to arrive," Wren said, waddling after him.

Liam snapped at his pregnant friend. "And just how the fuck do the police know to show up here? In case you've forgotten, there is no fucking service, and I am not sitting around, waiting to see if someone is going to come chop my body into tiny parts so they can put them in a fucking box under the tree."

He was breathing heavily, instantly regretting his words when he saw the sting on Wren's face.

"I'm sorry," he tried. "I'm just—"

But Wren shook her head. "No, it's okay. You're right." She wiped at the steady stream of tears as they slipped down her cheek.

Liam's face softened, the guilt twisting its way farther up his spine like poison ivy. He sighed but then turned back toward the hallway, swiftly making his way through the corridor and into the foyer. The roads were likely terrible if the state had shut them down, but he could at least sit in a locked vehicle, away from here, with the heat blasting.

If he made it that far.

He did one last double-take over his shoulders as his friends' pleas continued in the background, but then he stepped onto the rug by the entrance and looked up.

And then he screamed.

REBECCA
THEN

"Isla." Rebecca's voice was shaky as the wave of adrenaline began to crash, breaking on the surface of her cold, clammy skin before another tidal wave pulled in. "Isla, why isn't she crying?"

She stared at her friend, Isla's face wide and unblinking as she held Rebecca's baby.

"Isla!" Rebecca scrambled to push herself up farther, despite the delirious amount of pain, to meet her child and make sure she was okay.

If only she could've lived in that suspension forever, not knowing whether her child was dead or alive, and therefore, living with a snippet of hope and not the despair that would soon follow.

"Poppy," Rebecca said, her voice frantic. "Poppy, it's Mommy." She stared at her child in Isla's arms, not understanding what was happening. "Isla, give her to me."

But Isla didn't move, didn't budge a single ounce until Rebecca shoved her hands under Isla's, removing the baby from her grasp. Straw poked through the blanket beneath her, the reminder of their setting hitting in full force. They needed to call an ambulance as soon as possible now that she was keeping the baby, her mother's insurance be damned.

"Poppy, baby," Rebecca said again as she saw her daughter's face for the first time before instantly bursting into tears.

She is so beautiful.

Rebecca swiped a thumb across her daughter's puffy, cherub cheeks and then made her way to the tiny ringlet of curls on top of her head.

It was the same color as Rebecca's.

What she didn't understand, though, was why her eyes were closed or what that thing around her neck was.

Scarlett
Now

Scarlett's heart fell to the pit of her stomach at the sound of Liam's scream.

She rushed past Wren and Isla, nearly tripping on her way out of the living room door.

Gun, she thought. *I need my gun.*

Cursing herself again for giving the staff the night off, she vowed to keep her firearm and at least one maid on standby at all times after tonight.

If you make it past tonight.

She shuddered at the thought, rounding the corner into her foyer, the others just behind.

"What's wrong?" she asked immediately, temporarily relieved to see Liam unharmed. "Are you okay?"

But Liam's cries were his only response.

And then Scarlett saw why.

"Oh my God!" She gasped in terror, instinctively reaching for Liam's arm as all the oxygen disappeared from the room.

There, hanging by her fourteen-thousand-dollar chandelier that she'd insisted on having, was Carley.

And she definitely wasn't alive.

Wren bent over and hurled on Scarlett's Persian rug while Liam violently shook with tears, but all Scarlett could do was stare at her old friend.

Blood stains streaked across her purplish body, indicating she'd been dead for several hours, and puncture wounds pierced her skin. The most disturbing part, though, was her neck. Someone had impaled her throat, stabbing it through one of the wrought-iron prongs from the chandelier so her head was cracked backward at an unnatural angle, and the rest of her limp features hung stiff as a board as she dangled in the air.

What the fuck?

"I told you this wasn't a *fucking game*," Liam shouted at Scarlett, having regained his composure enough to speak. "Someone's here, and they just killed another person from our circle!" He fell to the floor, his tears descending with him. "Oh my God, I'm so sorry, Carley. I'm so sorry."

Scarlett finally tore her gaze away from the horrendous sight and stared at Liam. His face was beet red as tears continued to slip down his face, and for the first time, she wondered if her ignorance had caused this.

If she'd called the cops yesterday instead of trusting her stupid husband, would they have been able to prevent this? If she'd told the others about what happened, would they have canceled or perhaps rescheduled when things were safer? If she'd opened up instead of keeping everything inside like she'd been conditioned to do her entire life, could they have prevented this?

Could they have saved Carley?

These were the answers she would never know, never formally seek, because she feared she knew them already.

"I'm . . . so sorry," she mumbled under a stunned breath, the world spinning around her.

"It's a little too fucking late for that," Liam sneered, his voice angry.

Scarlett opened her mouth to apologize again, to make him understand, but the sound of liquid hitting the hardwood floor distracted her.

"Oh, shit." Wren grabbed her lower stomach, her cheeks flaming red. "I'm so sorry. I pee when I get nervous, and . . . and this baby is always on my bladder." Her voice faltered as large tears shined on her face.

"It's okay," Scarlett said immediately, suddenly wanting nothing more than to redeem herself. "We have extra clothes—"

Her words were cut off by a moan that sounded a lot like pain as Wren winced, her mouth dropping open. Their eyes locked, and the realization hit the two women like an avalanche, slow at first and then plummeting to the earth, bit by bit, without any power to stop itself.

Wren's water had broken.

And she was in labor.

WREN
NOW

A RAPID PAIN SHE knew all too well spasmed in her lower belly.

No, she thought.

"No, no, no."

This isn't supposed to happen. Not here. Not like this.

"What's wrong?" Isla placed a hand on her shoulder, concern permanently etched into her brows.

Wren tore her gaze from Scarlett, looking at Isla as her stomach tightened. "I don't think I peed," she whispered. "I think . . . I think my water just broke."

She heard several intakes of breath as Isla and Liam gasped, all while Scarlett was cursing.

"Are you sure?" Liam asked.

Was she sure? She didn't know. She'd given birth four times already to her own children, but her water had never broken naturally. Every time she labored, she'd started with Braxton Hicks, then real contractions until it was time to go to the hospital, where they broke her water for her after administering an epidural.

"I think so?" It came out as a question, not a statement. None of them had biological children, so it wasn't like she could ask about their experiences. The realization hit her like a bitter force, and she audibly winced from the metaphoric pain.

"What are we gonna do?" she asked, her voice frightened.

She was only thirty-six weeks along. The chances of survival were high, but the baby would likely need intervention, NICU time. And it's not like anyone here was qualified to deliver a baby, and Wren would be damned if she were about to have this kid with no drugs. That was nonnegotiable for her when discussing the arrangement with the IPs, who, by the way, weren't even there!

Not to mention the dead carcass that swung from Scarlett's chandelier.

Talk about a nightmare before Christmas.

"The roads are still closed," Liam said, his common sense seeming to return. "Even the driveway is covered and likely iced over underneath. We have no way out." And then, "We're stuck."

Wren opened her mouth to respond, but she never got the chance.

Instead, the sound of glass shattering in the next room interrupted them all.

"What was that?" Wren asked, her voice reaching hysterics.

Scarlett's words stumbled out fast. "Considering Carley is dead, my bets are on Quinn Waterbury, or whoever the hell this person is, coming to kill us all."

"Oh, fuck, fuck, fuck." Liam grabbed his hair with both hands as he rocked back and forth like a small child.

Wren's face remained in shock, her natural instinct as caretaker falling to the wayside. "What are we gonna do?" she asked again, holding a hand to her ever-growing stomach.

"We need to hide." Isla's voice was low and rushed, and for once, Scarlett didn't disagree with her.

"Come on." She stalked to a door on her right, twisting the knob open quickly. "We need to get to the basement. It's safer there."

Without thinking, Wren obeyed, waddling toward the door and down the staircase in her wet pajamas, tears still staining her cheeks. This wasn't at all how this was supposed to go. The baby's mother was supposed to be here for the birth. They had a whole plan mapped out—a process to follow. And did she mention the *drugs*?

She stepped onto the carpeted landing in Scarlett's basement, which was modeled like a home theater, no less relieved than she felt upstairs.

This was bad, so monumentally bad. She had roughly twenty-four hours to deliver this baby before the risk of infection set in.

Another loud crash sounded from upstairs, and a chill raced down Wren's spine.

"Bastard."

Wren whipped her head around to see Scarlett staring at her handheld camera monitor. It's a wonder that thing still worked. "What is it?"

"He, she, they, whoever it is, they broke another window. Those things cost a fortune to replace."

Liam let out another hysterical laugh, saying what they were all likely thinking. "As if that's what we're concerned about right now."

Scarlett shot him a daggered look, then returned to the monitor, flipping through the screens. "I can't fully see them, but from the various shots, it looks like they're circling the west side of the house."

"In English, please," Isla said, grabbing the device from Scar's cold, hard hands before she promptly stole it back.

"They're going back and forth from the front door to the driveway." She tapped the screen with his long nails. "Dammit, this thing is so grainy. I can't tell who it is."

Another contraction began working its way through Wren's stomach, and she gasped, reaching for Liam's outstretched hand and squeezing it. The others continued to mumble to each other, but her panic drowned them out. How the hell were she and this baby going to *survive*?

"I have to get out of here," she blurted.

All eyes turned to her, and for a moment, no one said anything.

Then, absorbing her role as their natural-born leader, Scarlett spoke up.

"Okay. I have a plan."

REBECCA

THEN

Oh, no.

No, no, no. This cannot be happening.

She'd read about this in one of the online message boards she'd frequented over the last nine months.

Pale yellow.

Dangerous.

Wrapped around.

Rebecca had worried slightly about the baby's health while in utero, but more than anything, she'd been focused on keeping her pregnancy a secret for fear of abandonment. She was only nineteen years old, still in college, and currently living off a depleting student loan. She didn't have what it took to be a mother—she was sure of it, which was why she decided to turn the child over to a Safe Haven volunteer in secret. It was only when she knew she was about to meet her that Rebecca changed her mind, instantly knowing she would love this child too much to part with her.

Too bad love wasn't enough.

Tears splashed down onto her child's face as Rebecca understood what Isla must've figured out the moment the child slipped into her hands.

Poppy wasn't crying because she wasn't breathing.

Rebecca unwrapped the cord from her daughter's neck and cried, trying desperately to give her a fighting chance.

In the end, though, none of it mattered.

Because Poppy was dead before she even began trying.

ISLA

NOW

THERE WAS NO WAY this was happening.

She was not helping another friend give birth while stranded in a snowstorm.

The world wasn't cruel enough to replicate that nightmare.

"All right," Scarlett said, taking charge. "Wren needs to get to a hospital, and we all need to stay alive. I know the roads are bad, but I'm not hiding here like those girls do in the horror movies."

She walked to a large red painting on the opposite side of the room and removed it from the wall, revealing a safe. Isla watched in awe as she swiftly opened it, dug her hand inside, and then flung a set of keys at Liam.

"These are the spare keys to Calvin's truck, the white Dodge in the driveaway. It's a full-size with four-wheel drive, so we'll take that. Liam, you drive. I'll sit in the back with Wren in case she needs to push. Isla, you take the front. When we get to the main road, I'll talk to the police, send them back here to investigate. I know the roads are bad, but we'll just have to go slow and hope for the best."

It sounded like a good starter plan, Isla thought. But that's all it was, a plan. And if there's one thing she knew, it was that plans didn't always go according to plan.

She cringed as the reality of the moment hit her. How had they gotten to this point? Just moments ago, her biggest fear was her friends finding out she lied to them about Rebecca's secret, and now, Wren was in labor, Carley was dead, and their stalker-murderer had come for the rest of them.

But why?

Was it Quinn?

Her brain still couldn't keep up with that rationale. They'd bullied her, yes, but not so extensively she'd come back to murder them all.

It's her, her mind whispered. *The one who brought you all here tonight.*

Her eyes popped open, and before she could control the thought, she blurted, "Scarlett, why did you invite us here tonight?"

The question must have thrown her off because her face twisted in confusion. "What are you talking about?"

Isla wasn't backing down, though, her conviction growing stronger by the second. "It was your idea to have the Secret Santa party here. You sent your entire staff away for the night, and your husband is suspiciously absent. Now Carley's dead, and suddenly, you want to thrust us all into a truck together during a deadly blizzard?"

She wasn't buying it.

While there was still a possibility that Quinn or another outsider was doing this to them, the odds of it being Scarlett were all the more convincing. She'd always been conniving and ruthless, the most likely one out of the group to commit murder.

If they were taking bets, Isla would put her money on Scarlett every time.

Scar dropped her hands from her sides and stalked toward Isla, the same way a predator would when tracking its prey. "I don't know what you think you're implying, but you're out of your damn mind if you think I killed two of our best friends."

"Oh, please," Isla sneered, a false confidence in her tone. "Don't act like you loved Bec or Carley. We all know Wren is the only one in our group you care about. We've never really been friends, and you know it."

Her words were venomous and thick as they tumbled out into the air, but she didn't care.

This was a matter of life or death, and she wasn't about to let her high school bully stand in the way of her future.

"We may not all be hunky-dory, but I would never kill someone." Scarlett jabbed a finger into Isla's chest, making her fall back slightly. "You do whatever the hell you want, Isla, but I'm going to try and get us out of here alive."

Isla started to reply, but Liam cut in, causing her to bite her tongue. "If you two are done having it out, could we please figure out how the hell we're going to just walk outside and magically escape in Calvin's truck if someone is out there waiting for us? You literally said they're hovering between the front door and carport."

Scar held Isla's gaze for a moment longer, a question waiting in her quirked eyebrow. The tension was thicker than it'd ever been between them, but for the moment, Isla decided to cease fire and broke eye contact.

"Glad that's settled." Scarlett crossed the room, retrieving the security monitor again. She studied the screen, her face twisting back and forth in thought.

Isla saw her expression and butted up against her shoulder, trying to see what Scarlett saw.

It was dark outside, so the camera was in night mode. Scar had four screens playing at once, and Isla could just make out the all-black figure in the corner of one as they passed by the front entrance. Then, a moment later, she saw the person pacing the sidewalk in front of the driveway before they returned, repeating the same motion. She and the others watched for several minutes as they waited with bated breath, and Isla saw that Liam was right. There was no way they could just waltz out front, hop in a car, and leave.

"We need to create a distraction," Scarlett said.

"Like what?" Liam asked almost immediately.

"I don't know," she responded, licking her lips.

Suddenly, Isla had an idea. "We need to lure them to the other side of the house."

"Yeah, but how are we gonna do that?" Wren asked.

"Simple," Isla said. "We'll throw something through a window, like they've been doing. We'll cause a crashing sound to draw them away and—"

"And then we can sneak out to the truck," Liam finished.

Isla nodded her head, but Scarlett shook hers.

"They'll know it's a trap." She started pacing, stopping long enough to straighten a framed image of a movie poster. "It's too obvious. Why would a group of people who are being terrorized by a murderer-stalker cause an obnoxiously loud noise?"

Isla swore under her breath, knowing Scarlett was right. It was so hard to think right now. "Okay, then," she said after a beat. "What do you suggest?"

Scarlett stared at each of them individually, an uncertainty growing in her expression. Then, she took a gulp of air and returned her attention to the camera monitor, flipping to the foyer screen where Carley's carcass still hung.

"Her," she said, showing everyone the screen. "We need to burn her body."

SCARLETT
NOW

"ARE YOU CRAZY?"

Scarlett ignored Liam's dig. If they wanted to get out of here alive, they had to do something extreme, something drastic that would ensure they had enough time to make their escape. Anything less than would risk an unwanted encounter, and at least one of them would die. Scarlett wasn't going to let that happen.

They would not die by Quinn Waterbury's hand.

"That's the only way it'll work," she said, the plan formulating faster than she could think. "We need the smell of her burning flesh outside to draw Quinn away from this side of the house." She nodded, thinking it through as she spoke. "She'll freak out when she sees it and either run or try to put it out to stop the scent from traveling, especially with the cops stationed on Route 52." She nodded to herself, convincing her psyche this would work. "Either way, it'll give us enough time to make our escape.

She turned back to look at the group, fully aware of how vile this plan was. When no one spoke, she knew they sensed the repulsiveness of it, too. Nevertheless, it was a good plan; she knew it in her gut.

Now if only her same gut could stomach the execution.

Liam spoke next, his voice small. "Do you guys really think it's Quinn out there? I mean, if it is, I don't know. Maybe we could just *talk* to her instead of *burning* Carley's corpse." He threw his hands up dramatically, his voice hitting his signature high note. "Just a thought."

"It does seem a bit drastic, Scar." Wren's sentiment was quickly annihilated by the sound of her groaning through another contraction.

"We need to get Carley's body down, now," Scar said definitively, pulling her high pony down into a low bun as she spoke.

Of course she knew the idea was drastic. It was completely outlandish, but *she didn't want to die.* What about that did these people not understand? Was one dead body swinging like a pendant in her foyer and another chopped up in pieces not enough?

"How are we going to do that?" Isla asked now, wringing her hands. A nervous tick Scarlett had long ago picked up on.

"Well," she said, grabbing a pair of slippers from a nearby closet. "We'll need a ladder. Calvin has one in the garage. And something to roll her body up in to make it easy to carry."

"Someone knows an awful lot about disposing of a body," Liam said under his breath.

Scarlett blew a loose strand of hair out of her face. "I guess all those thriller novels I read are finally paying off."

Liam used to make fun of her for reading *genre* fiction, always acting like he was so much more esteemed than her for reading the classics and literary fiction. Guess the joke's on him now.

"Is there a tarp in the garage, too?" Isla cut in, diffusing the tension. "If so, we can grab both in one go. And we all go together." She surprised everyone with that last statement.

Glad someone finally came to their senses.

"I think so," Scarlett said. "The gardeners used some this past fall. I'm willing to bet they didn't throw them away like I asked." Calvin always hired the same shoddy crew.

"Okay," Wren said, her voice high. "Let's go. Let's just do it." She grabbed her stomach, yet again, gasping in pain. "I need a hospital—and drugs! I think my contractions are getting closer together."

Shit, Scarlett thought.

"On second thought," she said, "Liam, you stay here with Wren. Sit with her, help her through her contractions, and make sure she's okay. Isla and I will get the supplies."

She looked at Isla, hoping for a confirmation and feeling a small sliver of gratitude when she saw Isla nod. Their relationship had always been . . . complicated, for a lack of better terms, but none of that mattered right now.

"Come on," Scarlett said. "Let's go."

Isla immediately followed, but not before Liam grabbed her arm. "Wait."

Scarlett turned and looked at the two of them, trying to read whatever silent conversation was going on. She wasn't dumb enough to ignore that the two had stayed in touch over the years despite them both ghosting her the first moment they could. It was like one year passed without Secret Santa, and the dynamic of their friendship had changed forever. Becca went AWOL doing God knows what, Carley dropped out of college to *camp*, Isla moved to Ohio and transferred schools, and Liam took an internship in New York before graduating early. The only one left was Wren. Scar didn't mind too much at first, but once she realized some of the others had stayed in touch, that they were co-existing in a world without her, well, it'd bothered her more than she liked to admit.

"Scarlett?" Isla's voice broke through her pity party.

"Hmm?"

"Do you have a gun anywhere in the house? I left mine at home, but if you have one, we can try to grab it, too."

A divot of shock tried to shine through Scarlett's latest round of Botox. She hadn't expected Isla to be someone who approved of guns.

She gathered herself for a moment, deciding how much to divulge, when she said, "Why do you think I want to take the truck instead of my SUV?"

ISLA

Now

ISLA NEARLY GRINNED AT Scarlett's response.

"Okay, then," she said. "I'll follow your lead."

Scarlett nodded, swiftly moving toward the door. Isla stayed right on her toes and almost ran into Scarlett when she stopped abruptly.

"Wait." She swung her body back around, moved past Isla, and picked up the monitor.

Isla popped her knuckles while Scarlett double-checked the monitors, her anxiety climbing higher by the second. They had so much to accomplish, so much riding on this. No matter how hard she tried, she couldn't help but think about that awful night so many years ago when Rebecca labored in the hollowness of that nativity scene. The blood. The sweat. The tears. Isla could not go through that again.

She would do whatever was necessary to get Wren to a hospital.

"All right, I can't see their whole body, but it definitely still looks like she's hiding out by a window near the front door. The garage is adjacent to the driveway, so we'll need to be extra quiet going in." Scarlett handed the device off to Liam, then looked at Isla. "You ready for this?"

No.

"As I'll ever be."

Scarlett offered a curt nod, then resumed her way back to the door. Isla waved to Liam and Wren, then followed closely behind. Together, she and Scarlett stealthily tip-toed up the stairs into the hallway, quickly ran past Carley's dead body, then weaved through the rest of the first floor until Scar stopped in front of a door. There, she placed a hand on the doorknob, ready to twist it, but Isla stopped her in a moment of panic.

"Wait," she said, her heart beating wildly. "What if she moved? What if she's in there somehow?"

Scarlett stared at her, not saying anything for a moment. If this were a movie, this would be the part of the story where someone jumped out of a hall closet and slashed one of them, sending the other running back to the others.

But this wasn't a movie.

"We'll attack," Scarlett said simply. "We will not go down without a fight."

Isla nodded, resisting the urge to cry.

Without another word, Scarlett took a deep breath, then swung the door open.

Immediately, motion detector lights spilled on, causing Isla's heart palpitations to stutter as she grabbed the sleeve of Scarlett's top.

"There are no windows in here," she said quickly, calming Isla's frayed nerves. "They don't know we're in here, so just stay quiet, and we'll be okay."

Deep breaths, Isla. Deep breaths.

She released her grip on Scarlett and slowly made her way into the garage. After a quick scan, Isla determined they were alone, and she breathed a sigh of relief. She watched Scarlett's shoulders drop from her neck, apparently equally relieved.

"Tarps should be over there if we have them." She pointed to the right side of the room before running in the opposite direction. "I'll grab the ladder."

Isla stumbled over her feet, nearly face-planting.

"Shh!" Scarlett hissed.

Isla stifled a silent cry, scrambled back to a standing position, and tried again, vowing to lick her wounds later. Her eyes danced over the walls, not seeing anything at first, but then landed on a chest underneath Calvin's workbench. She ran to it then, careful to watch her steps.

"In here?" she called over her shoulder before tugging open the box. "Do you think one tarp will—"

Her words got lost in her throat as she covered her mouth, trying desperately to muffle her scream.

"Oh my God, what is it?" Scarlett sneered, immediately dropping the ladder, which clanged loudly, and ran to Isla's side. "Isla?"

But Isla couldn't speak. She was paralyzed by the fear and shock of seeing a dead baby's body staring back at her.

"Isla," Scar continued to hiss. "What are you so freaked out about?"

When Isla still didn't respond, Scarlett shoved past her, investigating the contents of the box.

"There's nothing in here but an old nativity scene Calvin's grandma gave us."

A nativity scene, Isla told herself as tears spilled down her cheeks. *It's just a nativity scene. It's not real.*

She took several deep, sobering breaths, still unable to communicate, when Scarlett clutched her shoulders.

"Hey." Her voice still commanded attention, even as a whisper. "Look at me."

Isla didn't want to, not at first, but after a gentle squeeze on both shoulders, she opened her eyes and stared straight into Scarlett's hazel orbs, every vulnerability laid bare for her to see.

"We're okay," Scarlett said. "You're okay."

Isla nodded as more tears slipped out. "I know," she finally croaked. "It's just, that baby . . ."

The words got caught in her throat again, the way they always did when she was at a loss for words. She could tell Scarlett. She could confess right then and there, tell her all about Becca's daughter, Poppy, and how they lost her that night and how Bec had made her swear never to tell, but once again, as she stood there, staring into Scarlett's intimidating gaze, she couldn't bring herself to do it.

The shame was too much.

"I was supposed to have a baby," she said instead.

"Oh," Scarlett said, a sudden softness overcoming her. She dropped her hands and looked back at the baby Jesus statue. "Oh."

For a moment, neither of them said anything. The fear and adrenaline mixed with Isla's shame and guilt, swirling around her like the eye of a storm ready to strike.

She didn't know how much longer she could keep it together.

But then Scarlett spoke, saying something unexpected.

"Me too."

Isla looked back at her again, the yellow lighting in the garage shaking as the winds howled outside. "What?"

Scar nodded. "Yeah. Had a miscarriage, right before Becca's funeral, actually. It was . . . awful."

She was staring off into space now, a solemn expression on her face.

"I'm so sorry," Isla said, a rush of cool air leaving her lungs.

Scarlett shrugged, biting the corner of her lip as unshed tears lined her lash line. "Yeah, well. What about you?"

Isla tried clearing her throat without making a sound. "I, uh, I didn't miscarry, but I've had four failed IVF transfers. The last one was also during Rebecca's funeral."

Saying the words aloud felt like a boulder had been lifted off her chest, a comet that had once stomped out her view of the stars and dulled her sense of feeling.

Because now she felt everything, all of it at once.

And it was too much.

Isla was seconds away from bursting into flames and sharing everything when Scarlett chuckled.

"I guess we're not so different after all." She patted Isla on the shoulder before quickly dropping her hand.

Isla wanted to say something, anything, to continue this moment of connection, but just as soon as it had come, the moment had passed.

"Come on," Scarlett said, picking up the tarp before heading back to the ladder. "We need to get back."

Maybe in another life, if they both got out of here alive, this moment would mean something, but right now, they had to survive.

Nodding, Isla turned, but not before stealing one last glance at the mock baby Jesus and shuddering.

REBECCA

THEN

AFTER HOURS OF CRYING, hyperventilating, and holding her dead baby to her chest, Rebecca felt numb. It was nearly dawn, and despite the cold air, she couldn't force herself to move.

"Bec." Isla's gentle voice floated to her ears again, no doubt another attempt to soothe her. "Bec, I think it's time."

And just like that, another stab of pain seared through her. She looked down at Poppy, eyes closed and face pale, and her lip quivered as she realized she'd never seen what color Poppy's eyes were. She'd always hoped they'd be mossy like hers.

"Bec?" Isla tried again, this time placing a hand on Rebecca's shoulder, causing her to flinch.

"I just . . . I can't," she whispered under a shaky breath. "I can't just . . . bury her. Say bye to her." She wiped more tears away before they fell on her daughter's ashen face. "Nobody even knew about her."

Isla was quiet for a minute while Rebecca continued to sit, paralyzed by her inexplicable grief. Silence greeted them in every direction, the soothing nature of the nativity statues long forgotten.

Finally, Isla spoke. "We can't stay out here much longer. People will be up soon. They'll ask questions. We need to figure out what to do with . . . her."

The last word came out choked.

Rebecca shuddered and held Poppy back to her chest, the weight of her loss in a perfectly imperfect little blob. All ten fingers and all ten toes completely intact, attached to her limbs in all the right places. The swirl of auburn hair that lay atop her head and the unwashed pattern of newborn blood splattered across her.

Her Christmas miracle.

Now dead.

Becca let out a labored breath as she tried to focus on what Isla was saying. She'd started mumbling again, insistent they get out of the cold and figure out a plan to *dispose of the body*, like her child was a sixty-two-year-old murder victim they'd stumbled upon and not her child she'd just given birth to.

A small wave of anger burned inside her, making her snap. "We're not getting rid of her."

Isla's expression was pained. "I'm so sorry. I didn't mean it like that." She paused, wiping her bloodied hands over her face. It looked like they'd been involved in a crime scene. "I just mean, you need to decide what you'd like to do . . . with Poppy."

Rebecca squeezed her eyes shut, unable to differentiate her grief from her anger. If only she knew how long she'd be sorting through these feelings for the many years to come.

201

Finally, she moved to stand, her body working slowly as the trauma it'd just endured made itself known, and she winced. The large Mary figurine stared back at her as she clung to her baby, and she felt like puking at the odd kinship she felt to the statue.

And that's when the idea hit her.

It formed so quickly in the fogginess of her brain that she didn't have time to stop and think about the repercussions it may have.

"I want to leave her here."

Isla scrunched her face in confusion. "What?"

Rebecca nodded, suddenly sure of her choice. "I want to leave Poppy here, wrapped in cloth, lying in a manger, just like Jesus."

With a look of confusion, Isla stood up, scratching the back of her neck. "What do you mean, Bec? We can't just leave a *baby* here."

"And why the hell not?" Rebecca snapped. "She's my child, and she was born here, at the stroke of midnight on Christmas Eve. She was reunited with Jesus on both of their birthdays." She swallowed the lump in her throat, her gaze empty as she stroked Poppy's tiny head. "It's only fitting."

"But her body will freeze, and people will find her!" Isla argued. "What if they report it to the authorities? And what if they trace it back to us somehow?"

"Let them," Rebecca said simply. "I have nothing left to lose."

LIAM
NOW

"THEY'RE TAKING TOO LONG," Liam said, standing from the floor where he'd been sitting criss-cross apple sauce like a fucking kid.

"I'm sure they'll be right back," Wren said as she winced from what Liam assumed was another contraction. "It's only been a few minutes."

"No." He shook his head, pacing back and forth with absolute nowhere for all his nervous energy to go. "It's taking too long. And I thought I heard a noise." He paused, wiping the sweat from his brow. "Something's not right."

"Don't say that," Wren begged, her face tight as she breathed through another contraction. "We can't think that way. I'm not having this baby without drugs."

Liam gave her an odd look. "I think the idea of a murderer abducting or killing your newborn would be scarier than delivering without drugs."

Wren snorted. "Said the man in the room."

Touché.

He resumed his frantic pacing, practically burning a pattern into the overly expensive floor. They were still hiding in the basement's home theater, but not even the smell of popcorn and leather chairs could calm his nerves. Death had not been kind to Liam's family, slowly digging its cloaked claws into their skin, pulling each into the darkness a tad too soon. Liam had always feared it would come for him, too, but he was determined to fight. Liam simply wasn't ready to die.

The sound of feet pattering against the staircase caught his attention, and he grabbed the nearby Oscar trophy that had Katharine Hepburn's name inscribed on it and aimed it high above his head.

Just in case.

"Get back, Wren," he said low, under his breath.

She responded with a resounding scream as Isla and Scarlett stormed through the door.

"Oh, thank God, you guys are okay." Liam released a shaky breath and thanked whatever deity was in control of this organized chaos.

"Wren, what's wrong?" Scarlett immediately dropped her end of the ladder and ran to Wren, leaving Isla to fend for herself.

Typical, Liam thought.

Although, he supposed Wren was pregnant, to be fair.

He grabbed the ladder from Isla and sat it on the couch, quite purposefully leaving damages in the process.

"I'm fine," Wren breathed through clenched teeth. "Just a strong one." Liam saw her gaze fall to the ladder before she added, "Why didn't you leave that upstairs?"

Isla and Scar exchanged a glance, and Liam realized they looked more shaken than before.

"Did something happen?" He tightened his grip on the supposed Hepburn award, fingers moist with sweat.

"No," they both said at the same time, making Liam think that something did, in fact, happen.

"Honestly, I didn't even think about leaving the ladder," Scarlett added. "I just wanted to get back to you guys. It's spooky out there."

Liam still didn't trust they were telling the truth, but he didn't press the issue. They had more important things to worry about.

Like not dying and all.

"Whatever." He released his grip on the trophy and scrubbed his palms against his jeans. "We're gonna have to carry the ladder back up, and since this lovely idea was Scarlett's, I think you should do the honors of pulling our dead friend's carcass from your darling chandelier, if you can manage."

He still thought the idea was ludicrous, for the record.

Scarlett's lips twitched, but she didn't take Liam's bait. "We're not pulling her off the iron hook."

"Wait, what?" Isla jumped into the conversation, her face still white as a ghost. Liam made a mental note to pull her aside and ask what was wrong later.

Despite the situation, Scarlett looked just as smug as always as she pulled an item out of her pocket. "I snagged the hedge clippers from the garage. All we need to do is clip the chandelier from the ceiling, and it'll fall. We can roll her and the fixture up in the tarp and carry them to the fire pit outside together. That way, no one has to . . ."

Her words hung in the air, and for perhaps the first time that night, Liam felt a small sense of gratitude toward Scarlett.

SCARLETT
NOW

NOW OR NEVER.

Scarlett took a deep breath, readying herself for what was to come. She still couldn't believe Quinn had turned this psycho—if it was Quinn.

"Okay," she said, whipping her head back to the others as they prepared to rush the stairwell. "Remember, we stick together no matter what, and no screaming, *no matter what.*" Her gaze flicked to Wren, who nodded fervently in agreement. She checked the cameras, a surge of panic flooding her system. "Where the fuck—oh thank God. There she is."

The black figure was piling up a stack of bricks by a tree in the front yard. Scarlett squinted, trying to see if she could make out any more details than she previously had, but the screen was still too pixelated and the person too far away.

Their figure did look slender, though. Perhaps too slender for a man. It felt like a punch to her gut as she remembered all the times she'd made fun of Quinn. She should've regretted it sooner.

She cleared her throat and looked back at the group. "Once we get to the top, we just need to set up in the foyer, and I'll work on hacking the chandelier off. Calvin installed it, so I'm sure it'll be easy."

The time for protecting her husband's reputation was past her.

She suddenly wondered if Calvin would help her burn a dead body for a chance to escape and save their lives if he'd been home tonight.

Doubtful, she decided.

He wasn't man enough for that.

"Then, we'll make our way to the back patio and set . . . we'll set her on fire."

Jesus. "Then we beeline for the truck. Does everyone understand the plan?"

Scarlett waited for everyone to nod, then took a deep breath and pulled the door open to once again lead them upstairs. Adrenaline pulsed through her veins as the fate of their existence hung in the air. She climbed the carpeted steps as Liam and Isla trailed closely behind with the ladder. Wren was mumbling something behind them, so Scarlett halted, turning around to check on her.

"I'm okay," she wheezed. "Just another contraction."

Dammit.

"How far apart are they?"

Wren shook her head, breathing through the pain. "I don't know. Ten minutes, maybe?"

Scarlett, Liam, and Isla all exchanged a knowing gaze as the panic set in. None of them had given birth, but they knew damn well that meant this baby was coming sooner rather than later.

"Let's just go," Liam said, his voice squeaky.

The group resumed their quick trek up the stairs and reached the top of the landing. Scarlett peeked into the hallway, then motioned for everyone to follow when Psycho Quinn didn't jump out.

She's probably waiting to throw a brick at your head.

She shuddered at the involuntary thought.

"How you doing, Wren?" Isla asked.

It took a minute for their friend to respond, but eventually, she said, "Fine."

Scarlett was at the entrance to the foyer now, and she pulled her shirt over her nose, worried Carley's carcass might have an odor. She shuddered yet again, then gulped as she stepped into the room, her eyes falling to her friend's gruesome figure. She allowed herself approximately ten seconds to gawk, and then she got to work with the others, wasting no time as they manifested their escape.

Once the ladder and tarp were ready, she gripped the frames' edges and placed a foot on the bottom rung.

"Wait," Isla said, triggering another wave of adrenaline in Scarlett's bloodstream. "That's gonna make a huge noise when it drops."

Isla walked to Scarlett, a grim expression on her face. Scarlett stared, searching her eyes for words left unsaid.

"This is our only option, Isla."

But Isla shook her head as she bit her bottom lip. "No. It's too risky. There's no telling what Quinn will do if she hears the crash. Are you really willing to risk it?"

But Scarlett still wasn't understanding. "But if we don't cut the chandelier down, then that means—"

"I know," Isla said, cutting her off. Her expression was grim. "I can do it. Her throat isn't lodged too deeply. I'll pull her off, and you guys can catch her."

Scarlett's gut twisted. "I can't ask you to do that." Even if they had their differences, even if Isla was the biggest thorn in her side, she couldn't imagine tasking somebody with this.

Especially these guys. Because despite their toxicity, they loved one another. These were her people.

"It's okay," Isla said, a sad smile reaching her face. "I've done worse things in my life."

208

ISLA
Now

JUST ONE MORE DEAD body.

Isla just had to dispose of one more dead body, and then she was done, *for good*.

Gripping the sides of the railing, she mounted the ladder and climbed for dear life.

Step one.

You can do this.

Step two.

Just don't breathe through your nose.

Step three.

Lives depend on you.

Something between a grunt and wince escaped her lips as she scrambled up to the top of the ladder and stared into Carley's dead, unmoving eyes, her head upside down from where the iron prong had impaled her neck.

Fuck.

This was so much worse than she thought.

From afar, Carley's neck wound hadn't seemed too gory, but up close, Isla could see the loose tendons and ruptured glands hanging out of Carley's throat. Isla stifled a gag, then tore her eyes back to the face, where she saw gargled bits of vomit stuck to her friend's mouth. Blood stains were splattered across her nearly purple face; the sight was truly horrific.

Isla squeezed her eyes shut, gulping in a deep breath and immediately regretting it as the scent of copper and iron hit the back of her throat.

Just grab the back of her neck and yank her off, and you'll be done.

She immediately snorted at herself as the hysteria began to creep in.

Easier said than done.

"You sure about this?" Scarlett's voice floated up to her.

Isla cleared her throat, responding with a quick, "All good."

She grimaced and prayed a silent apology to her friend before gripping the back of Carley's head. Isla attempted to shove the dead weight of her skull up and over the hook, but she wasn't strong enough. The muscles in her arms shook as she tried again, causing the carcass to sway.

"She's too heavy," Isla silently hissed to the others before nearly falling off the ladder.

"Careful!" Liam half-way yelled, running to her side.

Isla took a moment to steady herself. This was going to be much harder than she thought.

"Liam, can you lift her legs up? Maybe if we alleviate some of the weight, I can get it."

Liam looked like a deer caught in headlights. "I did not sign up to touch the dead body."

"Oh, for heaven's sake." Scarlett stalked past him. "Here, Isla. I'll do it."

Isla thanked Scar, then attempted once again to push Carley's body up and over the hook.

"Dammit," she said. "It's still too heavy." She looked down at Scarlett, then over at Liam and Wren. "Liam, do you think you could just put Scarlett on your shoulders? That way she can hold Carley up more, like by the midsection. I think I can do it then."

Liam mumbled something inaudible but obliged nonetheless. "Fine. Come here, *princess*."

"Bite me," Scarlett sneered as he bent down. She hopped on his shoulders, then held her arms out slowly as Liam stood. "Okay," she said, blowing a stray hair from her face. "Can you move a little closer?"

Isla waited as Liam took a small step forward, then another. Once they were close enough, Isla nodded at Scarlett, who grabbed Carley and attempted to cradle her like a small child.

"Hurry!"

Isla snapped into motion, moving as quickly as her body would allow her. She placed a hand between Carley's shoulder blades and pushed as hard as she could, nearly shouting when it moved.

"It's working!"

"Shut up and hurry!" Scarlett said, her voice strained.

Isla continued pushing against the dead weight while Scarlett held the opposite end. "She's almost off." Worried her head would snap off, Isla grabbed Carley's hair and shoved it forward, finally dislodging the body from the wrought-iron spike.

"Got it!" she called as the corpse slipped from her hands.

Scarlett dropped her arms then, too, and everyone watched as Carley's body fell to the floor, the sound of bones shattering filling the air.

Suddenly, a high Isla hadn't felt in more than a decade rushed over her, and she let out a silent squeal as the literal weight of her friend's murder fell away from her. Quickly, she stumbled down the ladder, almost slipping on more than one rung, and rushed to her friends.

"We did it," Liam said, eyes wide. "Holy shit, we actually did it."

Isla fell to the floor, too stunned to speak as the reality of what'd just happened washed over her. Her friends continued to murmur in the background, eventually pushing her to the side as they wrapped Carley's body up in the tarp, but Isla's ears were buzzing. It had been so long since she'd touched a dead body. She didn't even touch Rebecca's corpse at the funeral.

Eventually, someone shook her shoulder, and she blinked rapidly, realizing it was Liam. "Come on. We need to move before they come inside."

Isla nodded, slowly rising, testing the composition of her limbs as she went. When nothing caved, she applied more pressure and stood firmly, her mind and body numb.

The next few minutes passed by in a blur, like a montage playing around her that her brain couldn't process. Deep down, she knew what they were doing. That some member of her friend group had taken charge and led them through the house and out the back door onto the patio, that someone had doused Carley's body in kerosene and then struck the inevitable match that would send their friend's body into flames.

She knew all of that.

But still, she couldn't get her brain to fully process what she was doing, what she was taking part in. The only thing her mind could see was the searing visual of the spike sticking out of Carley's neck, skin ripped and bruised and bloodied. And the *feeling* of pulling her deceased head off that spike, the crunching sound it had made as she pushed harder at the end. And the sound of her bones hitting the floor, cracking inside her lifeless body.

It was a feeling that would reside in Isla forever.

"Okay," Scarlett said, jarring Isla from her alternate reality. "Let's go. We need to move before the scent travels."

The sweet, putrid smell of burning flesh began to curl into Isla's nose, and she shuddered, her senses reawakened. "Okay."

She followed the crew back inside, and adrenaline forced its way back into her system. She picked up speed, snaking her way through the maze of Scarlett's house, ready to make their great escape. In a matter of minutes, the scent had already begun filtering in through the broken windows.

Poor Carley, Isla thought. *She deserved so much better than this.*

Just like Becca.

They reached the front door, which was closest to the driveway where Calvin's truck was. The group stood together, waiting as the sound of four beating hearts pounded wildly in the silence.

"How do we know if they're out there?" Wren finally asked, her voice hesitant.

Isla looked at Scarlett, also curious.

Scar held a finger up long enough to pull her security monitor out and check the cameras.

God bless Scarlett for being wise enough to invest in wired cameras versus wireless.

"There." Scarlett's face lit up as she pointed at the screen. "It worked. She's out back, trying to put out the fire it looks like." She showed the others the screen, and together, they watched as the figure ran inside the house, returning moments later with a bowl of water. "Now's our chance," Scarlett said.

Isla's inner flight mode kicked in, the adrenaline rush sobering. This was her one shot at getting out alive, and she wasn't going to miss this opportunity.

"Y'all ready?" Scarlett asked, hand already on the knob.

Isla, Liam, and Wren nodded simultaneously.

WREN
Now

THE PAIN IN HER lower stomach was now crippling, but Wren still wasn't giving up hope of making it to a hospital in time for an epidural. Her friend, Alexis, had given birth naturally, and she said the holistic mommy bloggers all fucking lied about it not hurting.

Wren wasn't willing to try it.

She breathed through another contraction as she followed the others onto Scarlett's front porch, then trekked down the stairs and through the fallen snow. Something akin to a leathery smell filled the air, letting them know the stalker still hadn't extinguished the fire, and all at once, it hit her.

The severity of what they'd done.

She stopped dead in her tracks as the onslaught of emotions took over.

"Wren, we need to keep going." Scarlett grabbed her elbow, attempting to rush her forward, but Wren jerked her arm back.

"Don't any of you realize what we've done!" she sneered in response. Tears rolled down her face, nearly freezing against her cheeks in the process.

For a moment, everyone stared at her, the only sound the rustling wind and distant crackles from the fire.

"That was *Carley*. Not some stranger or detached corpse but *Carley*. Our friend since elementary school. The girl who watched *The Wizard of Oz* with us at sleepovers and braided our hair before football games. Don't any of you realize what we've done?" Wren bent over, placing her hands on her knees as the guilt consumed her. "She was someone's daughter. And we didn't even give her the chance for a proper burial." The last words came out in a whisper.

"Hey." Scarlett gently cupped Wren's face and forced her to look up. Wren didn't want to meet her gaze, but Scarlett's cold hand was plastered to her face. "I promise you, when we make it out of this, we'll have the biggest memorial in the world. Televised on every social media platform possible, okay?"

Wren's face pinched as another sob wracked through her, the nauseating smell of Carley's burning skin threatening her nostrils.

"But right now," Scarlett continued, her normally perfect features in total disarray, "we have to survive, okay?" When Wren didn't respond right away, Scar repeated herself with more force. "Okay, Wren? You hear me?"

"Yes, yes, okay."

Scarlett dropped her hand, and Wren took the opportunity to wipe the ice-cold puddles from her face. If they didn't get inside soon, she feared her body was in danger of frostbite.

Luckily, she didn't have to wait long, because Calvin's truck was only a few more feet away.

"Thank God," she whispered, bending over and clutching her knees yet again.

Optimism spread like wildfire throughout the four of them as Scarlett fished the keys out of her pocket yet again.

"We're really gonna make it," Liam whispered.

Wren's insides did a complete one-eighty as she welcomed this new reality. "Let's get the hell out of here."

Scarlett smiled, a wide Cheshire grin stretching across her face as she unlocked the truck. The group erupted in a series of silent "yeses" before Scar threw the keys to Liam. "Here. You drive."

He caught the flying metal. "Yes, ma'am."

"Here Wren," Scar said, pulling the back door open and offering her a hand. "I'll help you up."

Wren thanked her, then did her best not to scream as another contraction tore through her.

"I think they're getting closer," she said after the pain passed.

Scarlett didn't respond, just simply ushered her into the back of the cab. "We don't have any time to waste. Let's go, y'all."

Relief flooded through Wren as the cushioned seat and warmth enveloped her senses. She listened as Liam and Isla got settled up front, and although they still had a dangerous drive to navigate, her nerves began to thaw.

Until Liam tried cranking the engine.

LIAM
NOW

"No, no, no!" He tried turning the keys again, cursing when nothing happened. "Dammit!"

"What?" Isla asked.

When Liam didn't immediately respond, Wren began to sob.

"Liam, what's wrong?" Scarlett demanded. "Why won't it start?"

"I don't know! It just won't. The fucking truck won't start." He tried once again, slamming his palm against the wheel when silence greeted him. "What the fuck, Scarlett?" He turned around, spit caught in the corners of his mouth. "You sent us on a suicide mission!"

"I didn't know the truck wouldn't work!" she yelled back at him before throwing her body back against the seat. "Fucking Calvin. The idiot probably left his lights on again."

Liam stared at her for a moment, his face slack-jawed. There was no way they'd done all of this for nothing.

"Wait," Scarlett said, scrambling to the front and jabbing Isla in the temple in the process.

"Ouch, Scar!"

"Sorry," she mumbled, her hands rummaging through the glove box.

Liam's panic levels were rising by the second. "Are you going to pull a magic rabbit out of there? Tell us all our problems are solved?"

He felt delirious.

"No," Scarlett said. "No, no, noooooo! My gun. Where is my gun?"

Oh for Pete's sake.

Liam threw his arms up, frustration overtaking his anxiety. "This is all just fucking dandy. We burned our best friend's body so we could sit in a dead truck with no weapon. Way to go, Scarlett. Bravo. You've really outdone yourself."

Wren continued to wail in the background while Isla stayed silent.

"This isn't my fault, Liam!" Scarlett was searching the center console now. "Where did Cora put it? She knows this is where I hide it!"

"Wait," Isla said, finally speaking up. "Maybe the stalker did this."

Scarlett quit pilfering long enough to listen.

"Fuck me," Liam said, already jumping to conclusions. "We are so fucking stupid."

Because of course Quinn or Ted or Ned or whoever the hell this psycho was had thought of everything.

"What do you—mean?" Wren asked, attempting to calm herself.

"She probably worried we'd try this. Probably ruined all of our cars"—Isla looked at Scarlett's empty hand—"removed any weapons." Her voice trailed off, her gaze growing distant.

"We never even stood a chance," Liam whispered, tears slipping down his stubbled chin.

For a moment, no one said anything. They simply sat, realizing the fate of their unexpected doom as more snow fell to the dust-covered ground. The silence of the mountains had always been one thing that Liam admired about where he grew up—now he found it devastating, a means to an end.

"This can't be it." Liam looked at Wren in the rearview mirror, watching as she clutched her chest. "This baby—"

His heart ached for her as he listened to Wren's panic set in.

"I can't—" she tried again, this time clutching her throat. "I need—doctors—hospital—this baby."

Her words were coming out in sharp breaths, each one more punctuated than the last.

"Hey," Scarlett said, sitting back down. "It's okay. We're going to figure this out. It's going to be okay."

But Liam didn't know how this was going to be okay. Hell, he doubted any of them did. They were stranded in the middle of the woods and a killer was on the loose.

This might very well be the end.

"Wait." Isla's voice chimed, a possible beacon in the despairing silence. "Scar, do you still have your grandpa's four-wheeler?"

Liam's heart constricted at the thought.

Scarlett looked at Isla, a surprised expression on her face. "I do. It's in the barn."

And suddenly, there it was: the feeling of hope renewed.

"It can only fit two, though." Scarlett looked from Isla to Liam, then back to their poor pregnant friend Wren.

In an instant, Liam knew what they must do.

"One of us has to take her," Scarlett said, confirming his thoughts. "Assuming they haven't discovered and ruined that vehicle, too, one of us will have to drive Wren to safety and then bring back help for the two of us who stay behind.

219

As they sat there in the pitch-black, maddening silence of the worst winter storm this side of the mountain had seen in a decade, Liam knew his fate. "I'll do it," he said. "I'll take her."

Scarlett and Isla eyed each other, fear etched on their faces as they, too, knew this made the most sense. Liam used to race ATVs as a teenager, so by default, he was Wren's best chance at getting to a hospital safely in these conditions.

Isla placed a hand on his shoulder, her face as pale as the snow outside. "Are you sure?"

He nodded. "Yes. I can get her out." His gaze dropped to her hand. "Plus, y'all know I can't fight. We'd die in an instant if I stayed behind and that psycho attacked. You and Scar are the vicious ones."

Isla let out a humorless laugh, a single tear cresting the top of her cupid's bow. The next thing he knew, she'd wrapped her arms around him in a warm embrace, and Liam teared up as well, realizing this may be the last time he ever saw her.

Finally, she released him, taking a deep breath and leaning back.

He squeezed her hands and then turned back to look at Scarlett. "Where is the barn?"

"Just over there." She pointed to the back left of the property. "The tank should be full. I have it serviced regularly but never use it."

He nodded, then turned to Wren. "Can you walk that far?"

She gave him a desperate look but then nodded, closing her eyes as she did. "I can do it."

He nodded, staring out into the bleak midwinter night. "What about you guys?"

"Don't worry about us." Scarlett leaned forward again, taking the keys out of the ignition and sorting through them. "Here. The blue key is for the four-wheeler. Just take her and get the hell out of here. We'll figure something out until you get back."

An unspoken understanding seemed to pass through them, and in the moment, Liam nodded, silently forgiving Scarlett for all the misdeeds she'd done in his life, while simultaneously hoping she felt the same.

Something loud sounded outside, causing Liam to jump. "Fuck. Come on, Wren. Let's go."

She nodded fervently, then waited for Liam to get out of the truck and help her back down, but not before offering quick neck hugs to Isla and Scarlett that likely packed years' worth of emotions.

"I love you guys," she whispered as she pulled away and took Liam's hand.

"We love you, too," Scarlett said.

"Both of you," Isla added.

Liam offered their signature "I love you" hand sign, his heart shattering into a million pieces. They may have all been cruel to each other at one point or another throughout the course of their friendships, but in their own twisted way, they still cared about each other.

Still *loved* one another.

He nodded to them both, then turned back to Wren and linked arms with her as they set off into the night, praying the darkness would be enough to cloak them from the Grim Reaper.

SCARLETT
Now

"It's just us now," Scarlett said as she faced Isla.

Wren and Liam had already disappeared into the white cloud of snow as they fought to get Wren and her surrogate child to safety, leaving the two of them to duke it out with the killer for the rest of the night.

"Where are they?" Isla asked. "Can you see them on the cameras?"

Scarlett blinked, a melted snowflake sticking to her lashes, then pulled out her monitor. After a few moments of flipping through the screens, she found the dark figure running back inside to the kitchen, filling multiple bowls with water.

"They're still trying to put the fire out." She handed the screen to Isla and blew what she hoped was hot air into her hands, attempting to warm them. The temperatures were already below freezing when the night had started, but now, she'd bet anything they were reaching single-digit territory. The thought of exiting the truck made her skin tingle.

"So much for global warming," she muttered under her breath.

Isla looked up at her. "What?'

"Nothing." Scar shook her hands out and then rubbed them together again. "Come on. We need to get back inside before we freeze to death."

"What, so we can be sitting ducks?" Isla stared at her in disbelief.

Scarlett cocked a brow. "As opposed to what we are now?"

A beat of silence passed, and Isla huffed out an annoyed breath. "Fine. What do you suggest?"

Scarlett turned back to her house, the one she'd fought so hard to get, yet now would do anything to never have to see again.

"We could go back to the basement." Her voice sounded defeated, even to her own ears. "Or I have an attic." She ran her fingers through the top of her pinned-back hair, a damp feeling coating her hands from where the snow had melted on her scalp.

Isla sat with this information before responding. "Which is safer?"

Scarlett blew out a breath. "Good question." Then, she pinched the bridge of her nose, trying to think. "There's no way to escape from the basement if she finds us, so I guess maybe the attic. There's a small window up there, so worst-case scenario, we could climb out of it and jump if we needed to."

She didn't want to think about how far that drop would be.

Scar looked at Isla and saw a myriad of emotions pass across her face.

"Okay," Isla said slowly. "How do we get there without being seen?"

Her mind working frantically, Scarlett began to outline their next route. "There's a servant's entrance on the east side. We can take that, and it'll lead us right to the second floor. The attic entrance is in the hallway." Pausing, she glanced back down at the monitor, noting the hooded figure's appearance by steam where the flames had once been. "She's still on the patio, but it looks like the fire is out. We need to move now and quickly."

223

Without another word, Scarlett opened her door and slid out, praying this plan would be their salvation.

ISLA
NOW

ISLA CRACKED HER DOOR open, the frigid air kissing her skin.

She was still dressed in Scarlett's flannel pajamas, her socked feet nearly freezing. Too bad the killer hadn't given them a chance to dress warmer.

Biting away her bitterness, she followed Scarlett as they tiptoed around the house and into the servant's entrance. It was tucked underneath a makeshift hill that Isla wouldn't have otherwise noticed if Scarlett hadn't pointed it out to her.

She trampled down the fluffy, white-covered stairs and cringed as the wrought-iron gate scraped against the concrete when Scar opened it.

"It's okay," she said. "They can't hear. Too far away."

Isla cracked her neck to the side, then straightened her shoulders as Scarlett wedged open the door. Once inside, she shivered, letting her body readjust to the heat. She bent over and brushed the wet snow from her socks, then decided in a last-ditch effort to remove them so as not to slip.

"Careful," Scarlett whispered as she began climbing the stairs. "There's a broken one somewhere. Calvin never got around to fixing it and refused to let me pay someone."

Still moving, Isla glanced down, watching her feet carefully as she climbed. The staircase wasn't large by any means, but it felt like an avalanche as they made their way up. She tried her best to be quiet, but nearly every step creaked beneath her weight. The panic in her body was on high alert as she wondered where the intruder was, not wanting to risk asking Scarlett to check while they were en route.

"Almost there," Scarlett whispered, and Isla felt the hairs on her arms rise as she slid her foot onto the final landing.

Made it.

"It's right down here." Scarlett waved before breaking into a slow run as she made her way down the hall.

Isla followed, a wave of relief rushing through her as she spotted the attic string hanging in the dim light. "Thank God." She watched as Scarlett jumped, attempting to reach the cable. "Want me to try?"

Scarlett shook her head, then tried again. "I've almost—"

Suddenly, Isla had the same unsettling sensation she had each time her stalker had been watching her. The off notion that someone's eyes were tracking her, despite a lack of physical contact. Isla spun around, the epinephrine in her body nearing dangerous levels.

Behind her, Scarlett had stopped jumping. "Isla—"

She whipped her head back to see what was wrong.

"Isla, I don't feel—"

Her words were clipped as she tried to finish her sentence and failed, swaying at first and then collapsing onto the ground.

"No." Isla instantly dropped to her knees. "Hey, hey, Scarlett. Scarlett, stay with me." Isla patted her face, gently tapping at first and then growing stronger with each passing second. "Scarlett." She tried to say it louder this time, but suddenly, her vision blurred, if ever so slightly.

What's happening?

Fear flooded her nervous system yet again, and she tried shaking the feeling off while also visibly shaking her friend. "Scarlett, please! You have to stay with me—"

And then, suddenly, she was no longer in control of her body.

Her movements slowed, and she began to sway. She felt like she was underwater, desperately trying to run and swim faster, but the weight of the tide slowed her, causing her to grow tiresome and weak as her arms fought against the invisible force.

Somewhere in the distance, the sound of *something* evaded her. What was that? It was growing closer with every passing second, and suddenly, it clicked:

Footsteps.

She heard footsteps.

Mustering all the energy she could, she pushed herself back up on her arms, swiveling her head around to see who it was.

But she didn't get to look for long.

Because a pounding erupted in the back of her skull, and darkness clouded her vision, pulling her into a very deep slumber.

PART III

REBECCA
Now

"WELL, THAT FELT GOOD."

Damn good.

Rebecca smiled to herself as she stared down at the bludgeoned version of her former friends, nemeses, and roommates. It had been so cute watching them try to fight, try to orchestrate their little plan with Carley, but Rebecca wasn't giving up that easily. She'd been waiting for this day for a long time.

Although, she must admit she'd grown rather impatient waiting for the Mistletoe Martinis to kick in. The wolfsbane she'd snuck in should've made them pass out an hour ago. Her plan was to knock them all out, then isolate *her* from the others. She was the only one who was supposed to get hurt, and the others were supposed to freak out, wondering where she'd gone. Rebecca had to improvise when she realized the drugs weren't working effectively, but that was okay.

She had other options.

Smirking, she pulled out the duct tape from her back pocket and used it to tie up Isla and Scarlett's hands and feet. Once they were bound tight, she shoved a bag over each of their heads, ensuring there was enough air for at least Isla to still breathe.

If Scarlett died before she revealed herself, that would be a shame, but she needed Isla alive. Rebecca wanted her to know exactly who was killing her when Rebecca took the last breath from *her* lungs.

Oh, she couldn't wait to see the *look* on her face when Isla realized little Becca wasn't dead! She smirked and clapped her hands thinking about it—Rebecca was truly satisfied with how she'd pulled that one off.

It was surprisingly much easier than she expected to source a dead body that somewhat resembled her. Finding a short, white millennial woman whose face she could bust up was easy. Ensuring she had red hair was a bit trickier, but she had done it.

Satisfied with her work, Rebecca began the process of dragging each body into Scarlett's abandoned nursery, deciding the ambiance would be nice.

Appropriate for the situation.

"Cunts," she said under her breath as she pulled each woman into the room.

When she was finished, Isla was tied to the glider, and Scarlett was bound inside the crib. She took a moment to step back and pause, admiring her work. At first, she smiled, feeling accomplished, like she'd finally done something she'd set out to do. But then, a moment later, she started to feel the crack in her sternum—the same one that was always there, nagging at the back of her thoughts.

Poppy.

No matter how hard she tried to live life to the fullest, having processed her grief in her own unique way, she could never ignore the burn, the rip in her heart at the end of a quiet moment, the pain that burst from the cracks in her chest, burning her soul from the inside out.

Nothing had ever been the same since that night.

And it was all thanks to Isla.

Sensing her anger getting out of control, she shook her head and took a step back. She needed to be calm if she was going to fully execute the plan, after all.

Rebecca tossed her red ponytail behind her and double-checked the knots she'd secured to both Isla and Scar before retreating down the stairs and out the front door into the cool night air. She breathed easier outside, always had. And despite those twats trying to pollute it with Carley's burning flesh, she still inhaled, filling her lungs, once, twice, thrice before exhaling and feeling in control of her emotions once again.

As she unrolled her shoulders and took in the sensation of the cool, crisp air, her thoughts returned to Carley, and she felt an ounce of remorse about having to kill her. That was never part of the original plan, but when Carley spotted her at the airport earlier that day, Rebecca had no choice but to act. Carley was feisty and had a big mouth; she never would've cooperated.

And Rebecca simply couldn't have that.

So, unfortunately, she had to improvise, which of course, left a nasty clean-up. She'd planned to dispose of Carley's body in the woods, but when she called her guy for help, he suggested fucking with them all a little more, and honestly, it wasn't a bad idea. Rebecca still didn't understand how he'd managed to hang her body from the chandelier so quickly, but that's what men like Julio were for.

They were efficient and didn't ask questions. Rebecca had experience with more than a few guys like him, especially during her stint as a stripper.

Another whip of cold air rushed by, and her thoughts drifted to Wren and Liam. She knew they'd attempted to escape on an ATV, but seeing as Wren was about to pop and Liam's veins were laced with wolfsbane, Rebecca had sent Julio to rescue them. He had vehicles hidden all over the property, so she'd asked him to get them out safely. If they asked questions about why he was there, he had his secret affair with Scarlett to fall back on.

No harm, no foul.

Feeling a chill, she tucked her auburn hair back into her hood and returned inside the house to check on her victims.

SCARLETT
NOW

WHEN SCARLETT AWOKE, HER vision was fuzzy.

Blurred colors and images played before her, her eyes dancing as they adjusted to the light. It took her a moment to remember what happened, but then it did, all at once, rushing in like a falling star.

Her eyes widened as she took in her surroundings, realizing she was in her daughter's nursery. She started to scream, but that was also no use as she felt the sticky residue of duct tape covering her mouth.

Oh my God, she thought.

Without thinking, she tugged her hands up to her mouth, determined to pull it off, but that's when she realized her hands were bound, too.

And so were her feet.

She let out a muffled cry as the panic truly set in. Before, she'd been fighting with all of her limbs and body parts, fully capable of defending herself, but now? Now she was bound and gagged, tethered to the most painful spot of her home.

"It's a shame, isn't it?"

Scarlett's already terrified eyes nearly split out of their sockets at the sound of a voice.

A woman's voice.

Quinn.

She turned in the crib and peeked through the slats, trying to confirm that's who it was, but the figure was dressed in all black and facing the changing table on the other side. Scarlett couldn't get a good look at her.

"Your daughter would've loved growing up in this room."

Scarlett's heart pounded against her rib cage as the person spoke again, but not because of what she said.

It was *how* she said it.

Her tone was so familiar.

Scar's eyes darted around the room as she desperately tried to plot an escape, a dozen plans already formulating in her mind. First, she needed something to cut the duct tape with, and then she'd have to attack or make a run for it. Certainly, there was something sharp in this room . . .

Isla.

Another muffled scream escaped Scar as her eyes landed on Isla, who was also bound and gagged, her body tied to the glider.

"Oh, come on, Scar," the woman said, turning around and taking a small step into the light. "Don't pretend like Isla and you are besties."

Finally, the woman fully stepped into view, and Scarlett's stomach nearly dropped to the floor.

Because it wasn't Quinn Waterbury.

It was Rebecca Anders.

Their dead friend. Their dead friend they'd buried weeks ago and then earlier tonight found her remains in their Christmas boxes.

She was alive?

"Yes, yes, I know what you're thinking." Rebecca tossed her hands out in a casual gesture as she walked toward the bookshelves Calvin had installed. "But, Rebecca, you're dead! Rebecca, I went to your funeral. Rebecca, I opened a box of your hair tonight!" She laughed as she feigned a horrified expression and then picked up a cover with Noah's Ark on it. "It's funny how that works, isn't it?"

Scarlett whimpered, still not understanding but desperately wanting her friend to untie her, let her go, and explain all of this. What the hell was Rebecca doing?

"It's not as hard as you'd think to fake your own death, you know." Rebecca's voice sent another chill down Scarlett's back. "Honestly, Scarlett, I'm surprised you didn't figure it out, especially with how much you like to read those popcorn books." She paused, laughing a little as she traced the outline of the Bible character before carefully setting the book back on its shelf. "I was a little worried you'd figure it out, figure *me* out before it got to this point. But then again, you were never supposed to know it was me. Things got a little, shall we say, messy, tonight."

A cold sweat began to break out across Scarlett's back, and she instinctively tried to break free again, her wrists ringing from the pain when it didn't work.

Dammit!

"That's not going to work." Rebecca walked closer to her now, peering over the crib railing, inspecting her work. "You're too weak. How many martinis did you have again?'

Scarlett's eyes widened even more as the words sunk in.

Rebecca smiled again, a lethal gleam in her eyes. "Don't worry. It wasn't enough to kill you—unless you drank a shit ton. Just enough to make you all pass out. Or so I thought."

She winked and turned away, leaving Scarlett alone with her thoughts. How many drinks did she have? And what about the others? Is that how Carley died, too?

No.

It didn't make sense.

Oh my God.

She gasped as another thought occurred to her:

Wren.

Had she drunk any? What about Liam? Wren's was a mocktail, but who's to say Rebecca didn't also slip poison into hers? But who would do that to a pregnant person?

What if Liam passed out while driving? What if they die out there? What if the baby dies?

She squeezed her eyes shut as tear drops swelled in the corners.

"You're awfully quiet, Isla," Rebecca said, causing Scarlett to peel her eyes back open and turn to the side.

She watched as Rebecca stood over Isla, a look of hate plastered across her face.

And yet, Isla's features remained schooled. Despite their circumstances, she didn't look scared or angry. Her face was stone-cold still.

What the hell was going on?

"Don't feel like chatting? Catching up after all this time? Or have you simply forgotten how you murdered my child?"

ISLA

THEN

THERE SHE WAS.

The child Rebecca and David had conceived together, behind Isla's back.

They both thought they were so sly, keeping their affair a secret, but Isla had known all along. She saw them disappear together at that stupid frat party on St. Patrick's Day. When they didn't come back, Isla crawled up the stairs to the second floor, heavily wasted herself, and walked in on them having sex.

At first, she couldn't believe it. Thought she must have been seeing things, but then she saw Rebecca's head roll to the side on that awful bed, saw David's body thrusting into hers, and it was all too real. Isla had shut the door without either of them even noticing. Neither of them ever came clean.

When Rebecca came to her several weeks later, showing her the pregnancy test but refusing to say who the father was, Isla knew exactly what she wasn't saying.

Now, as she sat in the dug out of a nativity scene in the dead of night, Isla could see the tiny baby slithering out of Rebecca's vagina, and despite this child's innocence in the situation, she couldn't stop the wave of hatred that washed over her.

Lies, deceit, betrayal. Everything Rebecca and David had done to hurt her rose to the surface, anger overtaking her thoughts. She watched the small child writhe, trying to escape its mother's womb, and at that moment, she realized something.

She hated it.

She didn't want to, but she hated the child.

Perhaps even more than she hated Rebecca and David.

Another one of Rebecca's cries pierced the air, shocking Isla's senses.

"Come on, Bec," she said, clearing her throat and hopefully her hatred with it.

What was she thinking? The child was nearly out, and despite this being the hardest thing she'd ever experienced in her life, she couldn't blame the baby. She had to help it.

Except you don't, a sinister voice whispered inside her, and her hands froze as the child's head popped out.

Isla stopped breathing.

They cheated on you, the voice continued. *That child is a representation of the ultimate betrayal. She doesn't deserve to live.*

"She's here," Isla all but screamed, trying to quiet the evil that lurked inside her brain. She started to pull the baby out, but that's when she noticed it.

The umbilical cord wrapped around her neck.

Come on, Isla, it whispered. *She already came out half-dead. All you have to do is not . . . unwrap . . . the cord.*

240

Everything inside Isla froze as time stood still. Her body was both numb and roaring with rage at the same time, and she didn't know how to fight it. Didn't know how to stop the horrible voices inside her head telling her what to do. All she could see, feel, think in that moment was that neither David nor Rebecca deserved a child, a happily ever after. And that child didn't deserve shitty humans for parents, either.

She would be better off dead.

And so, despite everything in her body screaming at her to help, Isla remained still. She sat there and watched as Rebecca continued to push the small child out, never once making a move to unwrap the cord.

Yes, that's it, Isla. Give Mommy and Daddy the gift of a silent night, forever.

REBECCA
NOW

"Did you really think you'd get away with it?"

Rebecca crouched in front of Isla, staring straight through her russet-brown eyes.

"I knew something wasn't right about that night," she sneered, standing back up and relieving the pressure from her legs. "Once I was past the grief, the initial part of it anyway, I had this feeling in my gut that there was something I didn't know. Something you were keeping from me. Something that I missed."

The room was silent as she began pacing again, walking circles around the small perimeter.

"It took me years to figure it out. Countless restless nights, therapy sessions upended. Everyone thought I was crazy." She chewed the inside of her lip, warring with the rage inside her, willing it to hold steadfast until she could get this off her chest. "But deep down, I knew you'd done something, caused this somehow."

She paused again, turning slowly toward the woman who'd ruined her life, wanting Isla to see the vengeance in her eyes.

"It wasn't until two Christmases ago when I went to visit her, our spot in the manger scene, when I finally got my answers. I was sitting there, talking to Poppy the way I always do, when something shiny caught my eye. It was early, you see. Maybe around ten in the morning. I didn't usually go until after nightfall, but I couldn't stand it that day. For some reason, I had to be there sooner, earlier that year. Something was gnawing inside me to go visit my little girl from the moment I woke up that Christmas Eve. So I did.

"I went, and I sat there in that same little space, hoping but also not really caring if anyone saw me, and that's when the camera caught my eye."

Rebecca popped her jaw to the side, clenching her teeth as the rest of the thoughts poured out.

"I didn't notice it before—probably because it blended into the night, but there, in the daylight, I saw it plain as day. And you know, that just really got me thinking." She eased her gaze back down to Isla's, whose eyes still looked blurry from the lingering poison effects. "So, I wandered inside, curious to see if my theory was right. And right away, a lovely gentleman greeted me. Introduced himself as the priest, asked me about myself, and so on and so forth. You know how they can be.

"And so anyway, Father Robb and I got to talking, and I discovered they'd actually had cameras installed for years. Twelve years to be exact. So, me being me, I came up with some bogus story to convince him to let me sift through some old footage, and it worked! He led me back to a closet of old tapes right then and there."

The tension in the room cut deeper than the knife in Rebecca's back.

"It took a while to find it, but after a few hours of digging, I did it. I found the tape from that awful night when my Poppy girl was born."

243

Isla clenched her eyes shut, and Rebecca's insides roared to life.

This is it.

She took the remaining two steps to close the distance between them, crouching down again. Then, her voice came out in a whisper. "And do you wanna know what I saw?"

Isla's eyes popped back open, fear and water lapping like crashing waves over her irises.

"I saw you do it, Isla. I saw you deliver my baby, saw you stare at her wrapped-up little neck, doing absolutely nothing for way too long, and then you leaned forward, pinched her innocent little nose, and smothered my child to death."

SCARLETT
Now

SCARLETT COULDN'T MOVE.

Couldn't breathe.

Couldn't think.

Couldn't *exist* anymore with the knowledge she now possessed.

If what Rebecca just said was true . . .

Impossible.

"You *killed* her!" Rebecca's sudden rise in voice made Scarlett jump, nearly soiling herself in the process. "She was my daughter, a mere baby, and you killed her."

Isla whimpered in response, which only made Rebecca angrier. "It wasn't enough that your boyfriend raped me, destroying my life. Oh, but wait, you didn't know that part, did you?"

Oh my God.

Scarlett's mind raced as she thought back to that awful night she'd found Rebecca at that frat party. *David* had done this? He's the one who raped her? And it resulted in *pregnancy*?

A velcro-like noise hit the air as Rebecca ripped the duct tape off Isla's mouth. Scarlett still couldn't process what was happening, her mind buzzing from the adrenaline and traces of leftover poison.

"Becca." Isla's voice was shaky, her previously calm face now plastered with blotchiness and tears. "Becca, I had no idea—"

Thwack.

Rebecca backhanded Isla, cutting her off with the force of the blow.

"Shut up." She crinkled the tape into a ball and discarded it in the diaper pail. "I only removed it so Scarlett could hear it straight from the horse's mouth herself."

Scarlett's eyes latched onto Isla's, and in an instant, she knew.

She knew all of it was true simply by the look on Isla's face.

"I wasn't in my right mind. And I had no idea he raped you, please, you have to believe me." Tears flooded like a river as Isla spoke, but all Scarlett could think was: *You monster.*

A baby.

Isla killed a fucking baby.

She couldn't wrap her head around it.

"I was so jealous," Isla continued, urging someone to listen. "I thought you two were cheating on me. When I found out you were pregnant, I just, just—"

"You just what? Snapped? Decided to kill an *innocent child*?" Rebecca was yelling again, but that was no longer the source of Scarlett's discomfort as Isla cried and continued trying to speak.

"Please, I am so sorry, Rebecca. I have spent every minute of every day regretting what I did. It's why I stayed with David, tried so hard to be there for you after the birth until you stopped talking to me." Snot dripped from her nose, but she didn't stop. "I've been living in my own personal hell every day since that night. I prayed you and Dave would never know, never have to experience more pain than I'd already caused you two. Because I am so, so sorry, Rebecca. I am so sorry."

Scarlett's wheels were turning as she tried to rein in the plot twist she'd never seen coming.

The stalker incidents.

The hints.

The little clues all pointing to a Christmas birth.

It all made disgustingly accurate sense.

Suddenly, Scarlett no longer knew what she would do if she found a way to cut herself free.

REBECCA
Now

IT WAS GETTING HARDER by the minute to restrain herself from killing Isla. How dare she say *she'd* been in pain? That *she'd* been living in hell.

Patience, Rebecca, she reminded herself. *Patience.*

Killing Isla now would be too easy, too simple, too fast. No, what Rebecca wanted was for Isla to feel the years' worth of pain she'd felt. She wanted to pinch her fucking delicate little nose and bring her to the brink of death over and over again, only to let go and let her breathe, let her suffer and wish she really were dead, because anything would be better than that.

"You're such a stupid fucking cunt." The words slipped out of her, vile and rage spitting into the air. "And I'm going to kill you tonight because of it."

"Please." Isla's voice was hoarse from all the crying, and Rebecca smirked, knowing this was only the beginning of her torture. "Please, Rebecca. I'm so sorry."

Laughter shook from Rebecca's body. "Sorry. Sorry, sorry, sorry. She's sorry everyone, did you hear? Scarlett, did you hear that? Little Miss Isla Mae Ellis is *sorry* for killing my newborn in cold blood." She clapped her hands together, twirling on the balls of her feet as her theatrics rose. "Well, then I guess that just makes everything okay then, doesn't it?"

Isla tried to speak, but Rebecca slapped her again, cutting her off before she even had the chance. "I don't wanna fucking hear it." Then, remembering why she'd removed the tape in the first place, Rebecca threw her voice over her shoulder, adding, "I'm so sorry you have to watch this, Scar. Truly, I am."

And she was, for the most part. She didn't like Scarlett, never had really, but she knew this was going to be trauma the poor woman couldn't unsee.

She vowed to make it quick when it was Scarlett's turn to die.

Rebecca couldn't risk Scarlett telling anyone what she'd seen here tonight, but that didn't mean she didn't feel guilty about it.

Suddenly, a flash of headlights filtered through the room, and Rebecca's heart stilted. Who the fuck was that? Didn't they know she had vengeance to seek?

Annoyed, she pulled a gun out of her pocket and placed a hand on her lips, miming a hush sound to the girls. Then, slowly, she tiptoed to the window and saw a truck pulling into the driveway beside Calvin's.

"It's Malcolm." Isla's voice broke Rebecca's trance, and she immediately lifted the gun, pointing it at Isla. "I'm just letting you know. He knows I'm here. He knows we're all here. I texted him during dinner, before we lost service. I told him we were staying the night. He knows someone has been following me, so he's probably worried."

Rebecca absorbed this new piece of information, letting it process as she devised an alternative plan. The simplest option would be to shoot Isla and Scarlett now and leave. Malcolm was such a fucking sap, so wrapped around

Isla's deadly hands that he'd come running toward the sound of the shot in a last-ditch effort of heroism, only to discover the love of his life was already dead. Rebecca would have plenty of time to escape.

But that would also mean she'd forfeit her hours' worth of pain and torture. Which she simply could not do.

Formulating a new plan, she walked back to Isla and patted her down until she found Isla's phone tucked away in her bra. Rebecca's face cringed when she saw the amount of moisture on the screen. Boob sweat had not been part of the plan.

"Call him," Rebecca ordered. "I turned the cell boosters back on right before I tied you up. Tell him something did happen but that you're safe and at the police station now." She shoved the phone in Isla's face, clicking on the familiar green icon once the face ID unlocked. "If you say anything to alert him that something is wrong or that I'm here, I'll kill him and your mother after I'm done burying you."

Isla nodded frantically, blinking back more tears. Rebecca hit the call button, and she waited with bated breath as the phone rang. She turned and stared at him through the window, watching as he pulled out his phone and then slid his finger before holding it to his ear.

"Isla." His voice came out worried and loud through the speakerphone. "I'm outside here at Scar's, and it smells awful. Are you okay?" He started to open the car door, then added, "I'm coming inside."

Rebecca arched her brow even higher as she shoved the phone back to Isla, silently daring her to see if she'd misstep.

"I'm fine." Her voice was still too fucking shaky. Rebecca turned the gun sideways and pushed it to Isla's temple. "Just shaken up. I'm at the police station, actually. Something happened, but I'm okay. Can you please come get me?" She paused before saying, "I don't think I can drive right now."

Rebecca dropped her gaze to the phone, then the window as she watched Malcolm hop back in his vehicle.

That's right, little monkey. Run along.

"I'm on my way," he said. "Be right there."

"Thank you," Isla squeaked as the line went dead.

Rebecca retreated to the window one last time, ensuring their visitor actually left. The man apparently had a death wish if he drove all the way here during this storm. He must have taken the backside of the mountain. Poor sap.

"All right," she said a moment later. "That was a close call. We better get started before someone else interrupts us."

ISLA
Now

DESPERATION SEEPED INTO HER pores as Malcolm's truck trailed off in the background.

This was it, Isla told herself.

This was the end.

She only prayed it'd be quick.

Rebecca flicked her ponytail to the side and rolled up her sleeves. "I had originally planned to make this much longer, but given our little interruption, I think we should speed up our timeline a bit, don't you? It's only a matter of time before lover boy finds out you're not really with the cops."

Hope deflated in Isla's lungs as she watched Rebecca pick up a pillow from the crib where Scarlett was still tied up.

"I'm actually a bit pissed off this is all I get to do, but honestly . . ." She swept her gaze around the small room. "I think this is fitting. Especially considering Scarlett's loss. Consider it poetic justice, if you will."

Isla gulped as Rebecca raised the small squishy pillow, and just like in the movies, her life flashed before her eyes. Twirling on the cupcake ride at the fair with her grandpa. Kissing Malcolm for the first time in high school. Eating homemade cheesy potatoes with her mom, which she secretly hated but didn't have the heart to tell her.

All of it, in one instance, steamrolled through her brain, eventually landing on one montage of core memories: her friends' Secret Santa tradition.

And then the night that ruined it all and changed her life forever.

Poppy.

A single whimper escaped her as the pillow made contact with her face, and Rebecca pressed, adding pressure, slow at first and then increasingly fast. At first, Isla tried to accept it, wanted to even. This was what she deserved after what she did. But then biology and mother nature kicked in as her lungs fought for air, and she thrashed, banging her head from side to side as she began to suffocate.

Panic set in as Rebecca's grip only tightened, and there was no more air for Isla to breathe.

Suddenly, a bang sounded so loudly, so intensely, that Isla's ears rang. The pillow fell from her face, and she inhaled, desperately seeking air. When she felt like she had enough that she wouldn't faint, she raised her head, startled at the scene that lay before her.

"Scarlett," she breathed. Scarlett was still lying in the crib, but now, Isla saw she had a gun in between her hands.

And lying on the floor, surrounded by a pool of blood, was Rebecca.

Isla's mind reeled as she tried to make sense of it.

"How did you—"

"Calvin," Scarlett said, interrupting her. "He left a damn nail sticking out of the edge of the crib." She fumbled to rip off the tape from her legs, then her ankles, talking profusely as she went. "That fucking idiot. I can't even imagine what would've happened to our child if they'd slept in this—this *death trap* he built."

Isla's ears still rang from the shot, but if she had heard Scarlett correctly, that meant she would've cut the tape off her hands using the edge of a nail.

"How did you get the gun?" she blurted through the fog.

"She left it on the top of the railing when she got the pillow." Scarlett stood, her legs wobbly as she climbed over the crib and got her bearings. "I guess she thought I couldn't reach it. Probably didn't realize there was any possibility of me escaping."

She blew a hair out of her face and immediately set to work untying Isla, who was still dumbstruck, her senses floating in the abysmal aftershock of what had just happened.

"Scar," she tried, clearing her throat, relief flooding her chest. "Scar," she repeated, her voice louder this time.

Isla waited as Scarlett's hands stopped moving. It took a moment for her to fully lift her gaze, but when she did, Isla saw a new version of her friend. One that was raw, vulnerable, scared. Someone who would never be the same again.

This was Scarlett unhinged, and it rattled Isla to her core.

"Thank you," she finally mustered. "Thank you, Scar. You saved my life."

A tear slipped out of the corner of Scarlett's eye socket, and she looked away, wiping it quickly before continuing. "Yeah, well, you're lucky I don't believe in an eye for an eye." Her hands slowed as she moved on from Isla's feet to her knees. "Although, if anyone deserved it, it's you."

Her words came out in a whisper, and Isla's skin crawled. She didn't blame Scarlett for feeling that way, but it caused another thought to nag at the back of her skull, starting at the base and inching its way up until it entered her frontal lobe and blurred her already unsettled vision.

"Why did you—save me?" The words felt thick in her throat, but Isla had to know. Had to know what happened next, had to know what Scarlett was thinking and feeling. Had to know if she would tell the others about what had happened.

If she would tell them what Isla had done.

After a beat of silence, she repeated, "Why did you save me, Scarlett?"

There was a pitch change in her voice, and the words came out domineering, like somehow they had switched roles. Scarlett's hands froze at the sudden shift, a crumpled piece of duct tape hanging from her left palm.

"I couldn't let her kill you." Her words were eerily quiet in the small of the nursery.

Isla squinted her eyes, not buying it. Something inside her was screaming *danger*. "But you could kill her?"

Scarlett flinched at her words, then got back to work ripping off the taping around Isla's wrists. "I had no choice. You and I both know she would've killed me after you. She'd be too worried about me telling. I knew too much."

She knows too much.

Isla's eyes grew wide again, the thought vibrating against her skull. Scarlett had saved her, but as she pointed out, *she knew too much.*

"Scarlett?" Isla asked, her voice turning deadly. "What happens next?" The words were cold and rigid as they settled on her tongue. "When we leave here, what happens next?"

She waited for a response, but Scarlett didn't look up, and in her silence, Isla received the answer she feared the most.

"What happens when we leave here, Scarlett?" Isla was desperate for her friend, her savior, to say anything other than the conclusion Isla had drawn in her head. "Are you going to tell the others about what I did?"

Once again, Scar's hands froze. The insurmountable tension drew to a head as seconds ticked by, and Isla inhaled a sharp breath when a voice she hadn't heard in nearly a decade echoed in her thoughts.

Kill her.

SCARLETT
Now

Shit.

Shit.

Shit.

Shit.

Scarlett had fucked up, and she knew it.

She should've just kept her damn mouth shut, or at least recovered her features sooner rather than later once she realized what was happening.

Dammit, she thought.

Anything would have been better than that—hell, a fake "I'm in love with you and actually a lesbian" act would've made more sense, would've saved her some time before the authorities got there.

Anything other than the fucking truth!

Because of course she was going to turn Isla in. The psychopath had killed a sweet, innocent, newborn baby. *Becca's* baby. It was the most vile offense she could think of. Isla deserved to rot in prison for what she'd done. A part of Scarlett had considered shooting Isla instead of Rebecca, but she knew if she killed Isla, then she'd still have to fight the woman who'd bound and gagged her and likely planned to kill her. So Scarlett had chosen to kill Rebecca out of necessity, a will to survive.

She was so stunned by what she'd just done that she didn't think before untying Isla; her body had moved on autopilot before her brain could catch up.

And now, it looked like she may need to kill Isla out of necessity, too.

After what was definitely a beat too long, she finally glanced up, meeting her friend's malicious gaze.

And she knew.

And Isla knew that she knew.

Scarlett had never been the best Catholic, but she hated these women for making her a murderer.

Forgive me, Father.

Quickly, she cut her eyes to the side where she'd discarded the gun after shooting Rebecca. She should've kept it, should've been prepared for this. But how could she have after she'd just murdered a friend in cold blood?

Her eyes shot back to Isla, and in an instant, they were both gunning for it. Scarlett leaped from her spot on the floor as Isla lunged from the glider a millisecond later. It wasn't far, but the distance felt like miles at that moment.

Scarlett's fingers curled around the barrel first, a small sigh of relief escaping her lips in the process. All she had to do was—

"Dammit, Scarlett!" Isla's body slammed against hers, pinning her against the floor. "I can't believe you're making me do this."

Scarlett couldn't see Isla's face with her own smushed into the floor, but she could've sworn it sounded like she was crying.

"I never meant for this to happen. For any of this to happen." Isla's words came out clipped as she applied more pressure to Scarlett's arm with her own, eventually cutting off circulation until Scarlett couldn't hold on.

The sound of metal clanged on the floor, and Scar cried again, this time out of defeat and desperation. But then she got her second wind, and she hurled her body over in an attempt to take control, pin Isla down, and put up the fight of her life.

She had already beaten death once tonight; she could do it again.

Had to do it again.

What she wasn't anticipating, though, was for Isla to do the same.

Despite her attempt, Isla elbowed her in the chest, cracking a rib in the process. Scarlett screamed, and Isla shoved her off, accidentally kicking the gun under the crib in the process. Without thinking, Scarlett moved at warp speed, army-crawling across the floor to the cradle where her sweet baby was supposed to have laid, slept peacefully at night once they'd moved past the newborn stage. She had everything planned out from the moment she peed on that stick, never once imagining she would have a miscarriage.

With her heart beating through her chest, Scarlett shoved her arm under the crib but then screamed when a rippling pain shot through her bicep.

"I'm sorry, Scar," Isla said as she grabbed the hem of Scarlett's flannel pajama shirt, dragging her out and tossing her to the side. "I didn't wanna have to do this."

She continued to ramble on about something, but Scarlett couldn't hear it. She couldn't concentrate on anything other than the pain Isla had inflicted, as evidenced by the footprint on her arm. A hot wave radiated through her humerus, and she was sure it was broken.

Run, she told herself. *You have to run.*

Scrambling to stand as she fought through the pain, Scarlett fled the room while Isla's head was still under the crib. She knew she didn't have much time, seconds maybe before Isla grabbed the gun and then chased her down.

Pain continued to shoot through her body as her arm felt like it caught fire, but she didn't stop. She had to keep going. Had to hide somewhere until she could escape.

"Scarlett!" Isla's voice echoed throughout the house just as Scar was rounding the pivoted staircase in the servant's hall.

Adrenaline pulsing, she flew down the stairs. All she had to do was make it to the door without falling, and then she could hide in the—

Dammit!

Three steps from the bottom, her foot betrayed her as she tripped on the broken stair, and she fell just seconds before a gunshot sounded behind her.

Tears ran down her eyes as she tumbled, but a shred of hope remained as she landed in the door's open entryway. Snow hit her face, and the cold sent a new wave of shock through her senses, willing her to continue.

Out of options, she plunged her body into the snow, hoping, praying, that it was enough to cover her as she crawled through it. The storm had picked up over the last few hours, and she guestimated at least two feet of snow buried the yard—and hopefully, her with it.

Another gunshot blew through the air, and Scarlett did everything in her power not to scream as she slithered through the icy sludge. If she could just get a few more feet away, Isla wouldn't be close enough to detect her and would move on, assuming she'd crawled around the house, not *through the snow*.

Seconds ticked by like hours as Scar continued to barrel her way through the fallen blizzard, and when she felt like she couldn't go on anymore, she finally collapsed, her body pounding against the cold, hard ground.

She just had to survive a little bit longer.

A few more minutes.

That's all she—

ISLA

TWO MONTHS AFTER

ISLA STARED OUT HER window, admiring how the first blades of grass were already popping through the frozen tundra that remained from winter.

Nature was resilient in that way. Always fighting to break free of the darkness, giving birth to new life at the beginning of each spring equinox. Isla especially loved how fully the colors would bloom before giving way to the tides of summer, followed by the inevitable death of fall and burial of winter.

But thus is the circle of life.

After she'd found Scarlett attempting to hide in the snow, she'd almost felt a sense of peace putting the final bullet in her, basking in the warm knowledge that she'd been the one to put her out of her misery.

A thanks she would never get.

Something tickled in the small, swollen area of her belly, and she tore her gaze from the view of her farmhouse window to look down. The mommy blogs had all said she could feel kicks as early as ten or eleven weeks, but at fifteen weeks and three days, she had started to worry.

Another strange, yet exhilarating sensation fluttered in her lower abdomen, and she smiled, wondering if this was it.

"Malcolm," Isla called, turning back to their bed and walking over to him. He was still half-asleep, lying naked in bed. "Hmm?"

"I think I just felt the baby kick." Isla's face lit up with joy as she felt another slight flutter. "Here," she said, grabbing his hand. "Do you feel that?"

Malcolm rubbed sleep from his eyes and sat up, obliging her request to cradle her stomach. After a moment passed, he shook his head. "Nope, sorry."

Isla felt a small fraction of disappointment that he couldn't share this joy, this moment with her, but of course, she knew it was too soon for anyone else to feel.

"Sorry," she said, sighing with a small smile on her face. "You probably won't be able to feel anything for a few more weeks when he's stronger, but I definitely think that's what it was."

Malcolm dropped his hands from her belly and then opened a palm toward her, inviting her in. "That's great, babe. Now, come back to bed."

She laughed, dropping her head and falling into bed, admiring the slow, lingering kisses he trailed on her body in the process.

This all felt so good, like the way it was always meant to be.

Two months ago, Isla dealt with the sins of her past, accepting that the chapter of her life was closed, now and forevermore, as she moved on to the next one.

Framing Scarlett's murder on Rebecca had been easy, almost too easy, in fact. After she'd killed Scarlett, Isla banged herself up a bit and destroyed Scarlett's security cameras before calling 911 and telling them the entire fabricated story of how Scarlett had escaped and left her behind. How Bec had followed Scar outside, and soon after, Isla heard gunshots. And finally, how Isla had managed to get her hands free right as Rebecca came back to kill her, too. Isla put up the fight of her life, winning over Becca's gun and shooting her in an act of self-defense. The cops had bought every word.

Perks of growing up in a small town, where everybody knew everybody.

The real challenge, though, had been convincing Wren and Liam. Isla was a great liar, but the anxiety she felt as she recounted the fake version of events to both of them later at the hospital was almost unbearable. Thankfully, poor Liam was still so riddled by his own near-death experience helping Wren escape that he didn't ask much, and Wren was so exhausted from giving birth that she could only cry in response. Isla had thought it best to let them mourn in their own respective ways rather than drag anything out.

Of course, finding and destroying the tape from the church had taken some time, though, but in the end, Isla handled it, the way she'd handled everything in her life.

She smiled as the memory mixed with the tingling sensation Malcolm's lips left on her skin.

She was proud of her work.

Because, deep down, Isla had always known this was who she was. From the moment she stopped that baby from breathing, she'd unlocked a part of her that could no longer lie dormant. No matter how hard she fought it, tried to hide this darkness inside, it always leaked out. Always prevailed in the crevices of her mind, threatening to bleed into the other parts of her life. It only took an act of near-death to stop pretending otherwise.

After all this time, she'd accepted who she was.

She no longer craved the approval of others.

Malcolm's teeth scraped against her shoulder as he bit her skin, and she shuddered, knowing she'd finally found her comfort.

Her home.

WREN

NINE MONTHS AFTER

THE SHOCK OF ISLA's pregnancy had hit Wren harder than a thousand meteorites.

Despite her and Rebecca paying off that doctor to sabotage Isla's last IVF transfer, they'd never planned for her to sleep with someone else and get pregnant naturally after all this time.

It was the margin of error they hadn't accounted for.

Wren sighed as she dressed her daughter, thinking how it was a shame Rebecca would never get to see her grow up.

After a night of one too many bottles of wine, Rebecca confided in her about everything. The rape. The secret pregnancy. The nativity scene. How she lost her precious Poppy, and finally, the truth about how Isla murdered her baby. She hadn't believed her at first, but then Rebecca played the tape she'd swiped from the church, and Wren had gasped in horror as she watched everything Rebecca had told her play out.

She knew right then and there she wanted to help. Becca had shared how she hadn't been able to get pregnant after the birth, so Wren offered to be her surrogate. It was a generous offer, she knew, but the more she sat on it, the more she realized it wasn't enough. Wren could see the torment in Rebecca's face, and her resentment toward Isla grew. Initially, she tried to convince Becca to release the footage, or at the very least, send it to the police, but Rebecca had refused, claiming she didn't want Poppy's memory to be tarnished more than it already was. It was hard enough to live through it alone, she'd told Wren. She didn't want to share this experience with the rest of the world.

It was too vulnerable.

Rebecca wanted to take matters into her own hands, and so together, they began to devise a plan.

The Lord giveth, and the Lord taketh.

And their plan would've worked out perfectly if she'd gotten the wolfsbane dosage correct, a blizzard hadn't isolated them, and she'd not gone into labor. She'd cursed when she found out what happened the next day in her hospital room. The moment Wren saw Isla walk in with the police officers, she knew Isla had killed them both, leaving Wren without her best friends and Rebecca's child without a mother. Her sob story was so convoluted, it's a wonder anyone believed her.

"There, there, sweet girl. It's okay, Piper." Wren picked up the child she'd carried for nine months and soothed her like she was her own. "Mommy's here."

She held the baby to her chest, enjoying the feel of her perfectly smooth skin.

"You girls ready?" Brennan's voice carried into the nursery.

"Almost!" Wren grabbed a green bow from the top dresser drawer and wrapped it around Piper's little head, a beautiful complement to her amber-red hair. "There we go. You look so beautiful."

Piper laughed in response, her hazel eyes glistening in the reflection of the sun's glow.

"There's just one more thing Mommy needs before we go visit Auntie Isla at her new house with Uncle Malcolm."

Wren handed the child off to Brennan, then retreated to the kitchen where a lavender-colored protein shake sat on the counter.

"What's that?" her oldest daughter, Shiloh, asked.

"Just a postnatal shake I made for Isla. She's gonna need the extra energy now that she has a newborn."

It'd been tortuous watching Isla strut around with her large, swollen belly once she moved home, acting like she'd been a hero that night and how God had just blessed her with a little miracle baby. And poor Malcolm—she had him wrapped around her filthy little fingers more than ever before. It was a shame he was going to have to become a single father, but in time, he would adjust, just like all men do.

"I still don't understand why I have to go to this." Brennan had strapped Piper into her car seat and was swinging the carrier, soothing her to sleep. "This sounds like a chick thing."

Wren plastered a smile on her face, ready for the day to be over with. "I told you, hun. The invitation said it's a co-ed Sip and See, which means spouses are expected, too."

Brennan scoffed. "What are we gonna do? Sit there and stare at Isla and the baby while we all pretend it's not weird as shit?"

"No, of course not." Wren rolled her eyes, grabbing the shake from the counter. "We'll all stare at each other as *we* take turns holding the baby. And drink alcohol. Perfectly normal."

She listened to her husband sigh, knowing he'd already conceded long ago when he originally agreed to go.

"Plus," Wren said, walking out the front door and digging in her purse for her keys. "I have a feeling this will be a fun party."

Brennan arched an eyebrow. "What do you mean?"

"I don't know." Wren shrugged. "Just a feeling I have."

She turned the key in the lock and then tightened her grip on the bottle. Conflicting emotions rattled through her bones. She knew it wasn't a mere human's right to determine whether someone lived or died. That was God's will and should be by his hand alone.

But in her defense, Isla started this.

There's a reason why women are called mama bears, and it isn't because they're cute.

The Lord designed mothers with an instinctive, primal need to protect their young, and somehow, deep down, Wren knew this was what she had to do, even if it meant sacrificing her own eternal destination.

Because that's what mothers did.

They sacrificed for their young, no matter the cost.

So, she would go to this party, and she would hand Isla the wolfsbane-laden shake—the proper amount this time—and she would sit.

And sip.

And see.

Because you don't fuck with someone's kids. That's just plain rude.

THE END

NOTE FROM THE AUTHOR

Hi, friends.

If you're reading this, chances are, you finished my book, so thank you so much for spending time with my words. This book was born out of many things—one being my disappointment when I discovered how lacking the Christmas thriller genre was when I set out to read one two years ago, and the other being the joy and nostalgia I found in my own Secret Santa traditions from years past. This book was meant to be a light-hearted popcorn thriller—an ode to one of my favorite memories, if you will. What it ended up being, though, was so much more.

Throughout this narrative, I began to explore mean-girl culture in a way I never had. I don't think I realized it at the time, but this was my attempt to understand why my friends and I subjected each other to cruel behaviors in the past.

My conclusion? We were all just trying to fit it. Be liked, loved. Or, in the words of Michael Scott, perhaps we all wanted people to fear how much they loved us. Because just like Gretchen Weiners in the classic *Mean Girls* movie, we all knew it was better to be in the "plastics" hating life, than to not be in it at all. While that doesn't excuse anyone's behavior, it certainly puts things into perspective.

And so, for that, I'd like to say *I'm sorry* to anyone I've ever harmed with my words. I know I wasn't always kind in high school, and sometimes even as an adult, I catch myself feeding into this toxicity. It's something the Lord is actively convicting me on, and I pray you'll find it in your hearts to forgive me. I also pray these new words will bring you closure and an understanding that my actions never had anything to do with you but rather my own insecurities.

Thank you,

Amy

ACKNOWLEDGEMENTS

Where do I even begin with this one? It's no secret this book was difficult to write, but thanks to the amazing village behind me, we finally got this thing wrapped up and delivered, sans body parts.

To my husband, Seth, thank you for always being my rock. You support me in more ways than one, and I'll always be thankful for that.

To my children, Willow and Ezra, thank you for simply being you. Mommy loves you with all her heart, and I pray you're never subjected to evils such as those depicted in this book.

To my mom, thank you for reading an early copy of this one and encouraging me when I was feeling down. Even more importantly, thank you for driving me to all those Secret Santa dinners way back when before I was old enough to drive myself. Oh, and for paying. Those Bath and BodyWorks lotions didn't pay for themselves.

To Danielle and Haley, honestly, where would I be without you ladies? Y'all are my rock. I had so, so many doubts about this book, and you were both there to listen and pick up the pieces the entire way. I love you both and am so incredibly grateful for your support and friendship. (PS—I hope you feel the same because you're both stuck with me regardless.)

To my alpha and beta readers, Rachel, Haley, Christina, Danielle, Alexis, Michael, Samuel, and Hannah, thank you so much for enduring the early drafts of this book. It was utter chaos, and y'all powered through anyway. For that, I am eternally grateful.

To my cover designer, Sam from Ink and Laurel, thank you so much for making all my wildest dreams come true! I've been dreaming of a thriller with one of your covers for ages, so this one really was special.

To my editor, Krys from Impress Millenial Books, thank you for your time on this project.

To my proofreader, Kaylynn, thank you so much for tackling this and catching all the errors. I appreciate you! Also, thank you to David for listening to me vent about this book, reading the horror-ish parts for a second opinion, and connecting Kaylynn and me!

To my narrator, Dana, thank you for taking a chance on this book! I feel so blessed to have connected with you and have adored hearing this story brought to life.

To Kristin and Ky, my PR rockstars, thank you so much for helping me market this book and managing my ARC team. You ladies made my life so much easier.

And lastly, to my friends, Tabitha, Justin, Kenedi, Whitley (and Nathan, because of course you're in all my books), and Chelsea, thank you for giving me so many fond memories. I already dedicated the book to our friend group, but you guys were the ones who stuck with me even after life caught up with us. I miss you guys and look forward to seeing what nickname we acquire in this next chapter of our lives, if given the chance.

Merry Christmas, y'all! And God bless.

ABOUT THE AUTHOR

Amy is a thriller author who was born in the heart of Appalachia before later relocating to the Midwest. With a Bachelor's degree in journalism and a professional background in content marketing, she has a passion for storytelling. When Amy's not writing, you can find her playing with her wild (lovable) children, hiding her book purchases from her husband, or rambling way too much on her Instagram stories. You can connect with her here: @authoramytackett.

Also by Amy Tackett

The Gala

The Tides of Our Sins

www.ingramcontent.com/pod-product-compliance
Ingram Content Group UK Ltd.
Pitfield, Milton Keynes, MK11 3LW, UK
UKHW041336281125
9257UKWH00034B/548